For more than forty years,
Yearling has been the leading name
in classic and award-winning literature
for young readers.

Yearling books feature children's
favorite authors and characters,
providing dynamic stories of adventure,
humor, history, mystery, and fantasy.

Trust Yearling paperbacks to entertain,
inspire, and promote the love of reading
in all children.

OTHER YEARLING BOOKS
YOU WILL ENJOY

THE CAPED SIXTH GRADER: HAPPY BIRTHDAY, HERO!
Zoe Quinn

THE CAPED SIXTH GRADER: TOTALLY TOXIC
Zoe Quinn

AKIKO ON THE PLANET SMOO, *Mark Crilley*

THE HERO, *Ron Woods*

THE IRON GIANT, *Ted Hughes*

SPRING-HEELED JACK, *Philip Pullman*

GLORIA RISING, *Ann Cameron*

ISLANDS OF THE BLACK MOON, *Erica Farber*

The CAPED 6TH GRADER

3

Lightning Strikes!

Zoe Quinn

ILLUSTRATED BY BRIE SPANGLER

A YEARLING BOOK

Published by Yearling, an imprint of Random House Children's Books,
a division of Random House, Inc., New York

If you purchased this book without a cover you should be aware that this book is stolen
property. It was reported as "unsold and destroyed" to the publisher and neither the
author nor the publisher has received any payment for this "stripped book."

Text copyright © 2006 by Working Partners, Ltd.
Illustrations copyright © 2006 by Brie Spangler

All rights reserved. No part of this book may be reproduced or transmitted in any form or by
any means, electronic or mechanical, including photocopying, recording, or by any information
storage and retrieval system, without the written permission of the publisher, except where
permitted by law. For information address Yearling Books.

Yearling and the jumping horse design are registered trademarks of Random House, Inc.

Visit us on the Web! www.randomhouse.com/kids

Educators and librarians, for a variety of teaching tools, visit us at
www.randomhouse.com/teachers

Library of Congress Cataloging-in-Publication Data
is available upon request.

ISBN-13: 978-0-440-42081-1
ISBN-10: 0-440-42081-4
GLB ISBN-13: 978-0-385-90306-6
GLB ISBN-10: 0-385-90306-5

Printed in the United States of America

September 2006

10 9 8 7 6 5 4 3 2 1

WITH SPECIAL THANKS TO
LISA FIEDLER

CHAPTER 1

IT'S sort of funny how, when your life is going along at ordinary speed, you can't help wondering when something exciting will come your way. Then, without warning, things start happening, and suddenly you're expected to be doing a thousand different things at once when all you really want to do is sit back and catch your breath.

I was thinking about that on Wednesday morning as Mr. Diaz marched the entire sixth grade to the auditorium for an assembly. All he would say was that he and the other sixth-grade teachers were going to tell us about a fascinating project that would begin the following week.

Personally, I've had more than my share of fascinating experiences lately, like finding out that I'm a natural-born superhero. It was pretty crazy at first, learning that I had powers and how to use them. Then there was the excitement of getting my very first supersuit, and taking the Superhero, First Grade test, which I passed with flying colors. (Literally! Amazing bursts of color actually flew out of the letter from the Federation telling me I'd passed.) The good news about that was that I didn't have to study anymore. The not-so-good news was that as a follow-up to the test, the Superhero Federation had given me a writing assignment: I had to do a report on my own heroic ancestry, researching my family's background and summarizing their experiences. Because it turns out I'm not the first superhero in my family; oh, no—in fact, there have been a bunch. It skips some generations, but both my grandpa Zack and his grandma Zelda were Supers too. That's a lot of superheroism for one family tree!

"I wonder what the surprise project is," said my best friend, Emily, as we waited in the hall with the rest of our class. She was standing near the tall windows that lined the corridor outside the auditorium. The day was bright and the sun made her black hair gleam.

"Me too," I said, glancing past Emily to admire the blazing blue of the sky. I couldn't help wishing I were outside, enjoying the sunshine. I imagined myself climbing to the top of the tallest tree on the playground (an easy trick for a kid with superpowers) and then jumping from the highest branch, out and over the school, over the parking lot. . . . It would be almost like flying!

Of course, I couldn't do this for two reasons. One: I'm supposed to keep my powers a secret. And two: flying wasn't one of my superpowers at the moment—but my grandpa Zack said it was one of the skills that often didn't develop until later on, so I was still hoping.

I felt someone nudge me in the back.

"Line's moving," said Howie.

I pulled myself out of my superdaydream and followed Emily and the others into the auditorium. The giant room was buzzing with chatter; everyone was trying to guess what the teachers were going to announce. Over the din I heard someone call my name.

"Zoe, over here!"

Josh Devlin was in the front row, waving to me. I could see that he'd saved some seats. I've had a crush on Josh for a long time, and lately, we've been hanging out more, so now Emily's convinced that he likes me, too. I nudged Emily and led her down the aisle; Howie came along.

"Thanks," I said, taking the seat next to Josh just as Mr. Diaz stepped onto the stage. He held up his hands and the roar of chattering sixth graders faded to silence.

"I'm happy to announce," he said in his booming voice, "that beginning next week, all the sixth graders from Sweetbriar Middle School will be taking part in a work-study apprentice venture."

Curious whispers rolled through the auditorium. I pricked up my ears—this sounded way more interesting than our regular school timetable.

"The object of this program," Mr. Diaz explained, "is to have you think about the sort of career you'd like to pursue in the future, then give you the opportunity to try it in the present."

Ethan Danvers, who liked to think of himself as the class cut-up, shot his hand into the air.

Mr. Diaz nodded at him. "Yes, Ethan?"

"Do we get paid?" Ethan asked.

There was a ripple of hopeful excitement. I looked at Emily; I could almost see her mind working, coming up with fashionable ways to spend her first paycheck.

3

"Sorry," said Mr. Diaz. "These will be strictly nonpaying jobs. This project is about observing, learning, practicing. These professionals will be taking you on as—"

"—apprentices," I blurted out loudly, before I could stop myself.

Mr. Diaz (and everyone else in the auditorium) turned to me. The teacher's eyes twinkled. "That's exactly right, Zoe."

So I was about to become an apprentice . . . again! Sixth grade was shaping up to be my best year yet!

"Here is how the schedule will go," said Mr. Diaz. "The project will take place over a two-week period. During those two weeks, you will report to school in the morning and attend regular classes until lunchtime. At lunchtime, you will be dismissed to go off to your apprenticeships, where you will spend the afternoon."

Allison Newkirk raised her hand. "I have saxophone lessons on Thursdays at three o'clock."

Some other kids chimed in, citing hockey practice, dance classes, and Computer Club meetings.

"Not a problem," Mr. Diaz assured the class. "You will be dismissed by your mentors at three o'clock, just as if you were at school. You won't have to miss any of your after-school activities."

Allison Newkirk looked relieved. I guess she must really love her sax lessons.

"You'll return to your homerooms at the end of school today," Mr. Diaz told us. "You will be given a packet of forms to fill out, and you'll have to describe the job you'd like to have. This will be an exciting chance for you to join the professional workforce and find out what we adults get up to all day!"

As we made our way out of the auditorium, everyone was

talking about the jobs they wanted. Emily, Howie, Josh, and I had study hall, so we headed for the library.

"I want to work as a fashion editor," Emily gushed, beaming. "And *Go, Girl!* magazine is published right here in Sweetbriar. I bet I could be an apprentice journalist."

"I hear they're looking for research assistants at the zoo," Josh said. "I'm gonna ask to be placed there. As an assistant to an assistant."

I thought that would be a great job for Josh, since he was into animal rights. And I was pretty sure he'd look really cute in green coveralls.

"I'd like to work with the police department," Howie said.

"Cool," said Josh, but I thought he sounded a little surprised by Howie's choice. *I* was definitely surprised. Howie had never seemed like the crime-fighting type to me, but then, I guess, neither had I . . . until I became a member of the Superhero Federation. So far I'd only caught a purse snatcher and helped bring an environmental bad guy to justice, but I never knew when I might be required to battle powerful villains set on destroying the world!

And now, along with my villain-battling responsibilities, chores at home, Super ancestry essay, and regular schoolwork, I was about to take on a part-time job.

WHEW!

So much for sitting back and catching my breath.

Emily, Howie, Josh, and I went directly to our favorite corner of the library. It's a broad alcove lined with windows, and it's far enough away from the circulation desk that Mrs. Cole, the librarian, can't hear us talking. Just as we were settling into our chairs around the wide rectangular table, Caitlin joined us. She flashed a glowing smile around the group.

"Hi, everybody," she said. "Is there room for me?"

Howie pointed to the empty chair across from him, and Caitlin slid into it.

Josh had already opened his binder and was scowling at an English worksheet. "Can someone please explain the present perfect tense to me?"

I'm great in English, but Caitlin piped up that she was an expert at verb tenses, and before I could say a word, she had scooted her chair over to help Josh.

"It's bad to have dangling participles," she said, pushing her hair back to reveal a pair of chandelier-style earrings. "Dangling jewelry, on the other hand, is always cool."

Without looking up, I rolled my eyes. Subtle? I don't think so.

Across the library I could see Suzanne Holbrook, an eighth grader and president of the Future Librarians Club, reshelving books in the reference section. She looked very serious as she guided the rolling cart along the narrow aisle between two tall, freestanding stacks. The cart was loaded with books; Suzanne plucked a thick volume about the Civil War from it and scanned the spines of the shelved books to figure out where it went. That reminded me . . .

"Be right back," I said. "I need to find a book about Ulysses S. Grant for my history report."

I got up from the table and headed toward reference, where I could see Suzanne reaching up to return a book to its place on the top shelf. Even standing on her tiptoes and stretching as far as she could, she was still a good six inches shy of the shelf.

It was as if I felt the trouble coming before it started to happen. I wasn't sure exactly what I was expecting, but there was something about the way my whole body began to tingle that told me I needed to be ready.

Suzanne was giving herself a knee up onto the top of the cart. She hesitated, getting her balance, then stood up.

The cart shimmied, then started to roll.

Well, duh! What did she think was going to happen? It was a *rolling* cart, after all.

The cart rolled out from under Suzanne, and her arms flailed desperately. Conscientious future librarian that she was, she didn't break the silence by shouting for help. Instead, she reached out to grab the freestanding bookshelf.

The shelf wobbled, and some books slid forward toward the edge. That was my cue. But first I needed to make sure no one was watching.

In superspeed mode, I glanced over my shoulder and saw that my friends were all looking out the window at the seventh graders having outdoor gym. Then I checked to see if the librarian was paying attention. Nope—she was stamping overdue slips. The coast was clear.

ZIP!

When I reached the reference section, I grabbed the falling shelf from behind and stood it securely upright, then stepped around to the front to catch Suzanne before she hit the floor. I

7

was a blur, so she had no idea I was even there, and in less than a split second, I was back at my seat in the alcove, just as my friends were turning away from the window.

Caitlin looked at me. "Where's the book?"

"Huh?"

"On Ulysses what's-his-name."

In the excitement of saving Suzanne, I'd forgotten to grab a reference book. I shrugged. "I couldn't find one," I said.

Then Josh said he was going to work on his history assignment instead of his English prep, which meant Caitlin wouldn't be giggling over him anymore. That was fine with me.

When everyone was involved in homework, I glanced over to the reference section. Suzanne Holbrook had gone back to shelving books. She had a weird look on her face, but I was pretty sure she wasn't going to mention her near accident to anybody. After all, the president of the future librarian squad certainly should have known better than to climb on a rolling book cart.

When the bell rang, we gathered our stuff and made our way out of the library.

"Zoe," Josh said as we filed through the periodicals section, "you never told us what kind of job you want."

"Hmm," I said, frowning. "I guess I didn't." The fact of the matter was that I had no idea what kind of job I could fit into my already crazy schedule. And since the project was about exploring future careers, I didn't see that there was much urgency for me. After all, I already know what I'm going to be—er, what I already *am:* a superhero.

We reached the corridor and headed off to our separate classes. By the time I took my seat in history class, I'd made a short list of apprenticeship options I'd like to try: astronaut, movie director, archaeologist. Of course, I had a feeling Mr. Diaz would have a tough time lining up mentors in those fields here in Sweetbriar. But then again, I supposed anything was possible.

And of course, there was always Speedy Cleaners, where, with Grandpa Zack's help, I'd be able to do my part to save the world.

I was pretty certain Mr. Diaz had never imagined *that* being part of the work-study project. Would he give me extra credit for it?

Probably . . . if only I could tell him about it.

CHAPTER 2

AFTER school I stopped by the dry-cleaning store to visit my grandfather.

"Hi, Grandpa."

He looked up from the cash register, where he was counting dollar bills. "Zoe, I'm glad you stopped by. There are some things we need to discuss."

Grandpa closed the register drawer and gave me a serious look. "I hope you've made some progress on your report for the Superhero Federation."

The fact of the matter was that I hadn't even started yet, but I didn't feel like talking about it, so I tried to change the subject.

"Don't worry, Grandpa, it's all under control. Hey, guess what? There's this cool project starting at school next week. It's a work-study thing. Every kid in the sixth grade is going to choose a job and then team up with a mentor."

Grandpa's eyes twinkled. "Sounds familiar."

"Yeah." I leaned my elbows on the counter and rested my chin in my hands. "I tried to think of a job I could do that wouldn't interfere with my superhero responsibilities. But if I have to take off every time there's an avalanche or a bank robbery, I think my boss is going to get pretty suspicious, ya know?"

"True," said Grandpa. "That's why most superheroes are self-employed."

"I know my Super stuff comes first. Still, I wouldn't mind trying out a really cool apprenticeship—regular, non-Super, but still cool. Like maybe a deep-sea diver, or a performance artist."

"Sweetbriar isn't near the sea," Grandpa reminded me.

"I know. And I'm not particularly artistic, either. So, got any ideas? But remember, it has to be something that won't keep me from Super training and heroic missions. Something with flexible hours."

"Uh, Zoe . . ."

I looked up at Grandpa. "Yeah?"

He sighed. "I'm going to be away. There's a weeklong superhero training seminar for Fifth Grade graduates. I've been asked to give a lecture on honing the power of superspeed. Gran's coming along. Those of us who are presenting are able to bring our spouses. She's looking forward to it. She hasn't seen Smokescreen's wife, Matilda, in ages. And she can't wait to see the photos of Laser Boy's new grandbaby."

"Smokescreen?" I echoed. "Laser Boy?"

Grandpa laughed. "He's almost sixty. I guess it's probably time for him to drop the *Boy,* huh? Anyway, his wife, Lucy, promised Gran she'd bring a whole album of baby pictures. And after the seminar, Smoke, LB, and I are taking the girls on an island cruise."

A prickle of worry began in my stomach. "How long is this trip, exactly?" I asked.

"Two weeks."

"Two weeks?" What was I going to do? Would I be able to handle my Super responsibilities without Grandpa Zack here to guide me?

"Yep. Two weeks." Grandpa clapped his hands together and hurried on. "Now, about that heroic ancestry assignment . . ."

"Wait a minute!" I said. "You're telling me I'm going to be on my own for two weeks? But what if . . . I mean, what happens when . . ."

Before I could manage a complete sentence, the door opened and in came Howie. His grandpa Gil, who owned the florist shop next door, was right behind him.

"Guess what, Zoe, Mr. Richards!" Howie's eyes were shining with excitement. "I'm going to be working for the SPD."

"Hear that, Zack?" Gil demanded smugly. "My grandkid's signed on with the Sweetbriar Police Department. He's going to be a real, honest-to-goodness crime fighter!"

"You sure found out quickly," I said.

"We Hunts have connections," boasted Gil.

"Actually," said Howie, "it was just a lucky coincidence. Mr. Diaz's wife plays tennis with Police Chief McCue's wife, so they know one another pretty well. Mr. Diaz called him on the spot."

"Congratulations, lad," said Grandpa Zack, reaching out to shake Howie's hand.

"Thank you," said Howie. "I asked Chief McCue if Detective Richards could be my mentor."

"The kid's going to be a natural crime fighter," Mr. Hunt said, glaring at me. "He can't wait to get out there and pound those bad guys into the dust!"

I seriously doubted that my father (or any good police officer) would intentionally allow Howie (or any kid) to get within miles of a bad guy. I hoped Mr. Hunt wouldn't be too disappointed when he found out that Howie would probably be doing things like answering nonemergency phone calls and pulling rap sheets.

"Guess what else," said Howie, who looked as if all his grandfather's bragging was beginning to embarrass him. "Grandpa is going to be a mentor, too."

"You, Gil?" Grandpa looked as if he was trying not to crack up. "A mentor?"

Gil shot Grandpa a scowl. "If you're thinking of the incident several years back when I was attempting to teach you-know-who how to operate that you-know-what . . . well, this is completely different. That you-know-what had double-intensified, turbo power-boosters, not to mention some very finicky state-of-the-art capabilities. . . ."

Grandpa cleared his throat loudly and Gil stopped talking fast.

"Caitlin Abbott is going to be his apprentice," Howie informed us. "Her application said she wanted to do something that 'celebrated the natural beauty of the earth,' and Mr. Diaz decided my grandpa's florist shop was a perfect fit."

"I'll be a fine mentor," Mr. Hunt grumbled. "What harm can come from teaching a kid to arrange fresh-cut flowers?"

I was pretty sure no harm could come from Caitlin's working in the flower shop, but c'mon . . . since when was she interested in the natural beauty of the earth? I knew her aunt Nina was all into health food and yoga, but Caitlin just seemed to

13

tolerate that stuff. It seemed weird to me, but I certainly couldn't say anything about it now.

"And what kind of internship will you be doing?" Mr. Hunt asked me.

"Actually," I said, shrugging, "nothing has really jumped out at me yet."

Mr. Hunt gave me a look that I couldn't really read. It was part pity and part satisfaction. "Well, I suppose you could always work here with your grandpop. You do spend a lot of time here. And after all, the world needs people who can get ketchup stains out of polyester blends."

Out of the corner of my eye, I could see Grandpa Zack scowl. I bet Mr. Hunt wouldn't say things like that if he knew Grandpa and I had the power to toss him up to Jupiter if we felt like it.

"As a matter of fact, I'd love to work here," I said, trying hard to keep the anger from my tone. "But Grandpa's going to be away, so I can't."

A moment of tense silence passed. Howie fidgeted uncomfortably, then broke the grim mood by announcing, "Grandpa Gil was just about to take me for ice cream to celebrate my job at the SPD. Wanna come?"

"Absolutely," said Grandpa Zack.

He turned the sign on the door to the side that said BE BACK SOON and we left—two humble, mild-mannered dry-cleaning professionals following Gil Hunt, florist extraordinaire, and his fearless crime-fighting grandson, Howie, down the street to the ice cream shop.

14

I was pleasantly surprised to find Emily arriving at the ice cream place just as we were. Allison Newkirk and Betsy Davis were with her.

"We wanted to invite you to join us, Zoe," said Betsy. "But we couldn't find you. It was like you vanished as soon as the dismissal bell rang. Poof!"

"Yeah." Allison giggled. "Are you, like, the speediest girl in the universe or something?"

"Maybe," I agreed, and Betsy laughed.

Howie and I introduced Allison and Betsy to our grandfathers and we all went inside.

Howie ordered first—mint chocolate chip on a sugar cone. The high school kid behind the counter reached into the glass case and dipped into the hard-packed tub of ice cream. He was wearing a T-shirt that said SCOOPER HERO. I got a real kick out of that.

Grandpa Zack ordered a root beer float, and I, of course, opted for my usual: a hot fudge sundae, heavy on the hot fudge.

Then it was Emily's turn. "I'd like a vanilla soft-serve, please."

Scooper Hero gave her an apologetic look. "Sorry. The soft-serve machine is on the blink today."

Allison and Betsy both looked disappointed.

"I was going to order soft-serve, too," said Betsy, pouting. "It's my favorite."

"Can you just try?" asked Allison sweetly.

The Scooper Hero shrugged and went over to the big stainless-steel soft-serve machine and gave it two hard thumps with his fist. Then he held a cardboard cup under the vanilla spigot and pressed on the plastic lever. The machine let out a pitiful mechanical growl, then made a sputtering sound. A pathetic dribble of vanilla ooze drooled out of the spigot and into the cup.

15

"Sorry, girls," the scooper said.

I took my sundae and a handful of napkins and joined Howie and his grandfather at a nearby table. The girls unenthusiastically scanned the freezer case for second choices.

The bell on the shop's door jangled, signaling the arrival of a new customer. *Hope whoever it is doesn't have his heart set on soft-serve,* I thought, turning toward the door.

The new customer happened to be the world's greatest comic-book author and illustrator: Electra Allbright! I was so excited, I forgot all about the soft-serve.

"Hi, Ms. Allbright," I called to her.

"Hello, Zoe." Electra scanned the room. "Why, look at all these sad faces!" she exclaimed, glancing from Emily to Allison to Betsy. "What's wrong? Don't tell me they've made sardine swirl the flavor of the day again."

"Sardine swirl was never a very big seller," the scooper informed her. "We've discontinued it."

"So why does everyone look so glum?" Electra asked, raising her neatly penciled eyebrows.

"The soft-serve machine isn't working," I offered.

"No soft-serve?" Electra sounded as if this were the worst news she'd ever heard.

"Sorry, ma'am," the scooper said.

Suddenly, Howie's grandfather was at Electra's side. "There's a frozen yogurt place over at Templeton Heights Mall. I'd be happy to drive you there."

"Oh, thank you, Gil," said Electra, bestowing on Mr. Hunt a glowing smile. "But I prefer ice cream to yogurt any day of the week." She turned away from Mr. Hunt and stared at the un-cooperative soft-serve machine.

16

Emily was pointing to a container through the glass. "I guess I'll have a mocha-toffee crunch," she said.

"Coconut for me, please," said Betsy. "On a waffle cone."

Allison was about to announce her consolation flavor when suddenly, the shop lights flickered and there was a loud zapping noise. I was so startled that the giant glop of hot-fudge-covered ice cream I'd just spooned up landed on the tabletop with a splat. I turned in time to see a shower of sparks shoot out from the back of the soft-serve machine. After a moment of silence, the machine sputtered, then began to whir contentedly.

"Whoa," said the scooper. "That's never happened before." He picked up a cone and cautiously held it under the center spigot, then pressed the lever. To everyone's surprise, a smooth, cool, creamy swirl of chocolate and vanilla ice cream appeared on the cone.

"Hey!" said the guy behind the counter. "It's working!"

Electra smiled at him. "Make that a large," she said, as though nothing out of the ordinary had happened. "Oh, and don't forget the sprinkles."

CHAPTER 3

HERE'S how it happened:

I was sitting there, frowning at the splat of ice cream I'd dropped on the table, when it occurred to me that if you squinted in just the right way, the melting ice cream looked exactly like a tornado wiping out a remote mountain village in Peru. And off to the side there were three little drips that looked just like superheroes rushing in to save the innocent people and llamas who lived there.

I was describing the image to Howie when I noticed Electra standing over my shoulder, munching on her ice cream cone.

"What a marvelous imagination you have!" she said. "Not only did you see an amazing vision in a hot fudge spill, but you described it vibrantly and with great style."

I felt my cheeks getting warm at the praise. I couldn't believe the greatest comic-book author of all time was complimenting me! "Thank you," I said.

19

"In fact"—she lifted her cone to me in a sort of toast—"you're super!"

"Wow. Um—thanks," I stammered lamely.

"Ever think of writing comic books?"

From his seat at the booth next to ours, my grandfather began to cough loudly.

Electra gave him a concerned look. "Zack, what's wrong?"

"Nut!" Grandpa rasped, then clarified quickly, "I had a nut stuck in my throat. But I'm fine now."

Electra turned back to me. "Really, Zoe. You should seriously consider the comic-book profession. And I'll be glad to help you out in any way I can."

Emily, who was halfway through her vanilla cone, began to bounce excitedly on the booth seat. "Zoe, this is perfect! You need a work-study job, and Ms. Allbright just offered to help you."

"Work-study?" Electra repeated.

"It's this awesome school project," I explained. "Our teacher, Mr. Diaz, is organizing it. We get to shadow a professional for two weeks and learn about his or her job."

"What a wonderful project!" Electra exclaimed. "I'd love to have a fresh, creative talent around my studio!"

"Really?" I wanted to jump up from the booth and hug her, but (a) I'd have looked dopey, and (b) she was still eating her ice cream cone and I didn't want to smush it all over her. "Thank you, Ms. Allbright! Thank you *so* much!"

"I'll call Marty—I mean, Mr. Diaz—right now to let him know you want to be my apprentice," she promised.

Smiling, she headed for the door, then turned back to wave good-bye to Mr. Hunt and Grandpa. I glanced over my shoulder and saw that Mr. Hunt had a broad grin on his face. Grandpa gave Electra a quick wave. He looked a little troubled. Not mad, exactly, just . . . concerned.

I was too excited to wonder why.

I was going to be working beside the world's greatest comic-book author, the person who created the coolest, most amazing girl-powered superbeing of all time—Lightning Girl!

The next day I was early for homeroom by a full ten minutes. Mr. Diaz was sitting at his desk organizing the work-study forms when I bounded in and nearly crashed into the bookshelf. He looked up and grinned.

"Morning, Zoe."

"Hi, Mr. Diaz."

"Early today."

"Uh-huh. Mr. Diaz, did you by any chance get a phone call from Electra Allbright yesterday afternoon?"

"Hmmm . . ." He stood and came around to the front of his desk, scratching his chin as though he were trying to remember. "Let me think. . . . Electra Allbright . . . Electra . . . Allbright." His eyes were serious as he seemed to search his memory. "Why, yes, I believe I did speak to a very nice woman by that name. Had a lovely chat, Ms. Allbright and I. You know, now that I think of it, I seem to recall that your name might have come up in the conversation."

"So I can do my internship as a comic-book author?" I asked, bouncing up and down.

"Absolutely! In fact, between you and me, I think it might be one of the coolest assignments in the bunch."

"Thank you, Mr. Diaz!"

"You're very welcome, Zoe. It sounded like you made a big impression on her."

"Well, I don't know about that. . . . She's probably doing it partly as a favor to my grandpa. They go way back."

Just then, the warning bell rang and kids started pouring into the classroom.

Everybody was still buzzing about the work-study project. When we were all seated, Mr. Diaz read off the list of students who'd already been placed with mentors. I was one of them, and so were Howie and Caitlin. Allison Newkirk was going to intern with a professor at the Sweetbriar Conservatory of Music, which seemed like a great fit to me since she was such a virtuoso on the violin. I was also really happy to find out that the editor in chief of *Go, Girl!* magazine had agreed to take on Emily as an intern (not as happy as Emily, of course—she actually screamed). Mr. Diaz didn't yell at her, though; he complimented her on her enthusiasm, then politely asked her not to do it again.

"That's about three-quarters of you accounted for," he said, finishing the list. "Those of you who haven't been placed yet shouldn't worry. It's just that the professionals in question weren't available to take my calls yesterday. I left messages for them, and I'm sure they'll respond by the end of the day." He took a stack of forms from his desk and began passing them out. "These are permission slips. Extremely important. They must, must, *must* be signed by a parent." He paused, then added, "Or guardian."

He wasn't looking at Caitlin when he said it, but we all knew he was referring to her aunt, since the rest of us lived with one or both of our parents.

22

I'd never had the guts to ask Caitlin where her parents were, or if something awful had happened to them. It just didn't seem right for me to pry. And besides, deep down, I feared the worst about the answer I'd get.

Sure, I had some weird hunches about Caitlin, but I knew I'd feel crummy if my folks weren't around, and I'd hate to think of any kid having to deal with that. Even an irritating kid.

"PSSST!"

I turned to see Emily holding a note. I nodded to let her know I was ready and she tossed it quickly across the aisle. I caught it, opened it, and had to stifle a giggle.

can you believe it? me, at GO, Girl! I'm gonna be such an awesome editor! maybe I'll win the cool-Litzer prize!

I snatched my pencil and wrote back quickly:

I think you mean the Pulitzer Prize.

I lobbed the note back to her. She smiled as she wrote her reply, then flipped it back to me:

23

That one, too!

As I tucked the note into my pocket, I had a feeling that if ever there was a kid who deserved a prize with the word *cool* in the title, it was Emily!

CHAPTER

4

ON Friday, Mr. Diaz confirmed that everyone had been placed with a mentor. And with the exception of Ethan Danvers (who'd requested an apprenticeship to the security guard of the main vault at the Sweetbriar Bank), everyone had gotten the job of his or her dreams. Ethan would be working at the ice cream shop, which had been his second choice, so he seemed okay with it.

After school, I went to Gran and Grandpa's to wish them bon voyage.

"Gran?" I called, going in through the kitchen door. "Grandpa?"

"In here, Zoe," came Gran's voice from the other side of the house.

I hurried through the living room and found her dragging some overstuffed luggage out of the bedroom.

"Here, let me." I dropped my backpack on the floor and slid my pinky under the handle of one of the heavy bags. "Where do you want it?" I asked, lifting the heavy suitcase with my little finger.

"You can put them in the trunk of the car, please."

"No problem." I effortlessly scooped up the remaining luggage—a giant duffle and a garment bag—in my arm and headed through the house.

"I'd almost forgotten how nice it was to have a hero around the house," said Gran in an amused voice. "Your grandfather hardly ever uses his superstrength anymore, unless of course he feels it's a real emergency."

"You mean like if he has to lift a major appliance because it's accidentally fallen on an unsuspecting repairman?"

Gran rolled her eyes. "I mean like if he has to open a brand-new jar of pickles. You know how your grandpa Zack loves his baby gherkins."

Gran carried my backpack as I brought the luggage through the kitchen and out to the driveway, where the trunk of Gran's powder blue convertible was already open.

Grandpa was carrying a fat scrapbook. I recognized it as the one he'd shown me the day I'd found out I was a superhero.

"Don't tell me you're bringing that on the trip," said Gran. "We've all seen those clippings a million times. And if you bring yours, I'm sure Smokescreen will bring his, and frankly, I just can't sit through that 'I accidentally set off every smoke alarm in the White House' story of his one more time."

"This is for Zoe," Grandpa said, handing me the book. "And it wasn't the White House, it was the Kremlin. I was there."

"And we had to dry-clean your supersuit six times before we finally got the smoke smell out of it."

I tossed the three bags in as easily as if they were cotton balls.

"NICELY DONE,"

said Grandpa, coming out of the garage.

"Thanks."

Grandpa turned to me. "You can use this book to research your assignment for the Federation. Pretty much everything you need to know about your Super genealogy can be found in these pages."

"People hardly ever use books as reference tools anymore," I grumbled. "Isn't this stuff on the Internet?"

Grandpa gave me a look.

I sighed. "Kidding. Just kidding."

"Be careful with that, Zoe," Grandpa advised in a somber tone. "Not only does it contain precious memories, but if it were to fall into the wrong hands . . ."

"I understand." The first rule of being a superhero is not to

28

talk about being a superhero. We can't have ordinary people finding out about the Super crowd. Who knows how the world would react?

"While you have that book, your superbackpack will be the safest place for it. Keep it in there whenever you aren't studying it. I think it's best if you keep it with you all the time."

Feeling a bit puzzled, I loaded the heavy book into my super-backpack, which, since I needed to keep my supersuit and tools handy, had replaced my ordinary schoolbag. "Why can't I just leave it home, hidden in my closet or something?"

"We can't risk letting your mom or dad find it. Why, if your father started flipping through that, he'd find out things about me he's never known."

"Well," Gran joked, "at least then he'd finally know the truth about why you missed seeing him as a talking mushroom in his third-grade play." She turned to me. "Grandpa was summoned to fight off a platoon of evil robots just as the curtain was going up. Zack hated having to miss the show. Brian was just the cutest little fungus."

I smiled and made a mental note to ask my dad if he had any pictures of himself in that mushroom costume. "Good thing we aren't going to be having homework during the work-study project," I observed, tugging the zipper of my backpack closed. "I'd never be able to fit this in with all my textbooks."

When Gran went back inside to see if she'd forgotten anything, Grandpa closed the trunk and leaned against the car's rear bumper.

"You realize you won't be able to reach me while I'm gone," he said.

"Yeah. I figured." I fiddled with the key chains on my back-pack. "I hope I can handle things on my own."

"I have no doubt," said Grandpa. "Now, listen to me carefully, Zoe. About Electra Allbright . . ."

"I'm so excited, Grandpa! If I learn enough during this work-study program, maybe someday I'll be a comic-book author, too."

"Yes, but I think you should know that—"

"Zack," came Gran's voice through the kitchen door. "Did you remember to pack the suntan lotion?"

"Yes," he called back.

"And the passports?"

"Got 'em." Grandpa turned his attention back to me.

Gran came out, closed the kitchen door behind her, and double-checked the lock. "Well, then, that's everything. Zack, we'd better get going—we have a plane to catch. Zip or no Zip—we'll never make it to the airport in time if we hit rush-hour traffic."

Grandpa looked at me as if he was trying to come to a decision. Then, with a sigh, he gave me a hug and got into the car.

"Be careful out there, kiddo," he said.

Gran kissed me on the cheek and climbed in behind the wheel.

I watched Gran back out of the driveway and waved as she drove away. "Have a good time!"

"You too," called Grandpa. Gran tooted the horn and they disappeared down the street.

Oh, I will, I thought, heading for home. *I definitely will.*

CHAPTER 5

I was surprised at how quickly the weekend went by. I'd expected time to drag since I couldn't wait to start my internship with Electra Allbright. But I was so busy that the days seemed to fly. I spent Saturday helping Emily pick out her "work wardrobe" for the next two weeks. Talk about a major mission— I bet there are superheroes out there who've never faced such an incredible challenge! I learned everything I will ever need to know about matching a belt to a purse.

For my hard work and dedication, Emily lent me her favorite sweater to wear on my first day as a comic-book author's apprentice. It was pale yellow with blue speckles, the colors of storm clouds and lightning.

When I left Emily's, I decided to cut through the small patch of woods that separates our neighborhoods to work on some superskills. I spent a good half hour climbing tall trees at superspeed, pretending they were skyscrapers. Then I pried a few enormous rocks out of the ground and practiced throwing them. Unfortunately, beneath the third rock was a slithery little snake. It was hard to tell which of us was more startled—me or the snake! I shrieked and tossed the rock over my shoulder, then turned and ran out of the woods at superspeed. I may be a superhero, but I still get pretty creeped out by snakes. They're just . . . creepy!

On Sunday, my parents and I rented some DVDs and hung out together, which was great. Before bed I worked on my Federation essay, using the scrapbook, careful to return it to my superbackpack when I was through. Then I dug out several old issues of Lightning Girl comics and quizzed myself on the details of her powers and her list of enemies.

In school on Monday, no one could really concentrate, so we didn't get much done in class that morning. Mr. Diaz just smiled as if he'd been expecting that.

Finally, it was twelve o'clock—time to head out to work!

I met up with Emily and Howie on the front steps of school.

"Hey, look," said Emily, pointing to a police car pulling up to the curb. "Zoe, it's your dad."

Sure enough, there was my father in the driver's seat of the Sweetbriar PD cruiser. I giggled, because I knew that detectives like my dad usually travel in unmarked cars and that he'd arrived in the one with the blue lights and the giant silver badge painted on the side for Howie's benefit. I glanced at Howie, who looked about as thrilled as I had ever seen him.

"There's your ride," I said.

Howie just nodded hard, smiling like crazy, and bounded down the steps toward the cruiser.

I waved to my dad, who was rolling down his window.

"Need a ride?" he asked.

"No thanks," I said. "It's nice out. I'll walk."

When Howie and my dad were gone, I turned to Emily and gave her a hug. "You go win that Cool-litzer Prize!" I said.

"And you go create an awesome comic-book adventure!"

"Count on it!"

I hoisted my backpack higher on my shoulder and headed down the steps.

I'd only seen Electra Allbright's mansion on the hill from a distance, but up close it was bigger than I ever could have imagined. On the outside, it looked like a cross between a fairy-tale castle and a giant birthday cake, with lots of unexpected porches and balconies and turrets with pointed roofs that were shingled with blue slate. It was exactly the sort of place a person as mysterious and creative as Electra Allbright *should* live.

I was reaching for the lightning-bolt-shaped knocker when the door swung open and there stood Electra.

"Zoe! Right on time."

"Hello, Ms. Allbright."

"Come in, come in!" She swung her arm in a welcoming gesture and I stepped into the high-ceilinged foyer.

"Here, let me take that backpack. . . ."

"Uh . . . well . . . it's really . . ."

Electra easily lifted the pack from my shoulder.

". . . heavy."

Electra paused, then quickly put my backpack on the gleaming

33

marble floor. "Yes. It is quite heavy, isn't it?" She gave me an extra-bright smile. "So, are you ready to get to work?"

I picked up my backpack (easily) and returned the smile. "Yes, ma'am."

"Good. Studio's upstairs."

I followed her through the front hall and up the broad, winding staircase, taking in the half-emptied moving boxes, ladders, paint cans, and drop cloths strewn throughout the living room.

"Pardon the clutter," Electra said cheerfully. "I'm still moving in."

When we reached the first landing, I could see that the upstairs hallway was being redecorated. The walls had been stripped and had a gritty, chalky look to them. Stacked in the corner were several rolls of wallpaper.

"Cool!" I cried, noticing the pattern.

"Like it?" Electra picked up one of the rolls of paper and unrolled a section.

"I love it!" I ran my fingers over the crisp paper, which was printed with hundreds of little lightning bolts! *Glittery* lightning bolts! The sunlight coming through a tall window above the stairs made each bolt twinkle. I would love to have my bedroom walls covered in a pattern like that one! When my mom redecorated the dining room last year, she lugged home about a trillion wallpaper books, and none of them had anything as cool as that.

"Where did you find it?"

"I had to custom order it," Electra answered. "It was between the glittery bolts and glow-in-the-dark ones."

"I'm glad you went with the glitter," I said.

"Yes, the glow-in-the-dark just seemed a little too trendy."

I laughed. I was positive that Electra Allbright was the only grown-up on the planet who would ever pick out wallpaper like that.

At the end of the hallway was another, less elaborate stairway, which brought us to her attic studio. For a minute, I just stood there, taking it all in.

"WHOA."

"Pretty terrific, huh?"

I nodded. The room was enormous—it was one huge, open space, the width and depth of the whole house, with extra-high ceilings and several windows. Some of the windows were oval, others were diamond paned, and still others were made of stained glass. The studio is sparsely furnished, with one wide, flat table and two smaller ones like desks with tops that can be adjusted to tilt upward. There were two sturdy office chairs and a big, comfy-looking one upholstered in a lightning-bolt-patterned fabric—another custom design, I was sure. Shelves hold sketch pads and other artist's tools.

On the bigger table was a large piece of heavy paper, like a poster. When Electra saw me looking at it, she explained, "That's a storyboard."

The storyboard took up most of the tabletop; it was a rough sketch of an entire book, with all the ideas and actions either drawn or written into consecutive blocks. Electra explained that when the comic book was produced, this one large board would become several comic-book pages. This technique allowed her to see the whole story play out at a glance on one enormous page.

"So," I said, unable to contain my enthusiasm any longer, "where do I start?" I had visions of Electra teaching me how to draw Lightning Girl—I'd always wondered how she achieved that perfect almond shape that made Lightning Girl's eyes so distinctive. Maybe she'd let me come up with a new and unique supervillain. . . . Now, *that* would be a challenge!

Electra tapped her chin with her finger. "I think I'd like you to arrange my colored pencils."

"Oh." That didn't sound like much of a challenge. "Um . . . okay."

I put my backpack down and Electra pointed me toward a cupboard. Inside was a large plastic box filled with colored pencils in varying lengths and degrees of sharpness. The pencils were in every color I could imagine—and a few I couldn't. Beside the box were a bunch of smaller, empty containers.

"Bring the box and those empty ones over to my worktable," Electra suggested. "We can chat while we work." She pulled the extra desk chair up beside hers and we took our seats.

"We're supposed to start off by asking questions," I said, suddenly feeling shy. "Do you mind?"

Electra laughed. "Of course not. That's how we learn. By asking questions."

"Okay." I put the pencil boxes on the table and sat down. "Did you always want to become a comic-book author?"

"Not exactly," Electra said. "I had other . . . um, career aspirations. But even while I was pursuing those, I was always a doodler."

"A doodler?" I giggled, thinking of my school notebooks, which, lately, I'd been covering with little hearts and a certain name. "I'm a doodler."

"I noticed!" Electra grinned. "So, who's Josh?"

38

My eyes grew round with surprise. "How did you know about . . . I mean . . ."

Electra motioned to my backpack. My social studies notebook was sticking out, and it was plain to see that the whole cover was decorated in various versions of Josh's name—bubble letters, block letters, script. . . .

"Oh." I felt my face getting warm. "Yeah. Josh. Well, he's . . . he's . . ."

"A special friend? A secret?"

I shrugged, smiling in spite of my embarrassment. "Yeah, I guess you could say that."

"Well, don't worry. I'm good at keeping secrets."

Suddenly, I was eager to get back to the topic of comic books. "How do you get your ideas?" I asked, hoping it sounded like a very professional inquiry. "Do you know what's going to happen from the start, or does it come to you as you work?"

"Oh, there's always a story in my head. All the different pieces of an adventure are swimming around in there, like memories."

"Memories?" I thought back to Lightning Girl's last adventure and wondered how Electra—or anyone, for that matter, besides Grandpa Zack and, well, *me*—could have a memory of tunneling to the core of the earth to douse a volcano. I supposed Electra was just making a comparison.

"Anyway," she continued, "it's really just a matter of taking the different elements and putting them in a proper, exciting, story-like order."

"Sounds difficult," I said.

Electra nodded. "Chronology is always the toughest part."

It was quiet for a moment. Then Electra picked up a black marker and uncapped it. "Now, about those pencils . . . I'd like

39

you to put all the red tones in one container, all the blues in another, then the greens, and so on. Got it?"

"Sure," I said, hoping that I'd eventually get a chance to use those pencils to draw an actual Lightning Girl scene. But if I had to start with sorting them, I was going to sort them the best I could. I wondered if I had any supersorting powers I could call on.

I reached into the large box and pulled out a sky blue pencil, then dropped it into one of the empty boxes. The next one was bright red, like fresh strawberries; I put it in a different box.

The third pencil I grabbed was a green one. Well, actually, it was sort of a greenish blue. Or maybe it was more of a bluish green. It reminded me of a mermaid's tail. Green-blue, blue-green. Okay, so did it go in the green box or the blue box? So much for supersorting.

I stared at the pencil for a long moment.

"More complicated than you thought it'd be, hmmm?" Electra said, not looking up from the background she was sketching. I could hear the smile in her voice.

"Yes," I admitted.

"That's one of my favorite things about color," she said, her marker moving swiftly across the page. "So many possibilities, so many subtle mysteries. Colors are complex, they can be more than one thing—kind of like people."

I'd never thought of it like that before. "I like that!" I said, rolling the bluish greenish pencil between my palms. "But I'm still not sure which box to put this in."

Electra glanced up from her drawing and checked the pencil.

"Let's call that one green-blue," she said. "I see a touch more of the cobalt tone in it, so put it in the blue box. Somewhere in that box you'll find one that's similar, but with more of an emerald tint."

"When I find that one, I'll put it in the green box, right?"

Electra smiled. "Color . . . such a wonderful way to learn the concept of compromise!"

After that, I picked through the pencil collection and Electra explained to me some of the technical aspects involved in drawing and producing a comic book.

"I don't go in much for all that computer-graphic stuff," she said, using the side of her thumb to smudge and blend the edge of a sketch. "I like good old-fashioned art."

Before I knew it, the clock on her desk (with the lightning-bolt-shaped hands!) was striking three.

"Zoe, would you mind seeing yourself out?" asked Electra, fishing through the red box for a raspberry-colored pencil. "I'm in the middle of a great thought and I don't want to lose it."

"Sure thing," I said. "See you tomorrow."

"Looking forward to it."

I grabbed my backpack, made my way downstairs, and closed the front door behind me. When my feet hit the front walk, it was all I could do to keep from breaking into superspeed, I was so excited.

Electra Allbright was looking forward to seeing me!

Man! How cool was that?

I'll tell you how cool that was: supercool!

CHAPTER 6

AT home, I had a marathon IM session with Emily. She told me all about her day at the magazine. I probably should have gotten a jump start on my chores for the week, but it seemed that the whole sixth grade was online and wanted to share their first-day news.

Howie was the only one who wasn't online—knowing him, he'd stopped at the video store on the way home and rented every police movie ever made, just to bone up on the lingo.

I stayed on the computer until Mom called me down for dinner. I could smell something spicy and I knew what we were having.

"Tacos. Awesome!" I slid into my chair and happily began to pile shredded cheese and tomatoes into my corn tortilla.

"How was your first day on the job?" asked Mom, handing a bowl of chopped olives to my dad.

"Well . . ." I scanned the table for the taco sauce. "It was good. Electra was drawing a really cool background page, and she told me all about how comic books are made while I sorted pencils." I bit into my taco, remembering the blue-green/green-blue issue. "It was way more complicated than you'd think."

"Sounds like you learned your first lesson about grown-up work," said Dad. "Even the little things can be challenging."

"And important," Mom added. "In any profession there are a million small jobs that can make or break the end result."

"Even if you're just sitting there at a desk for hours, sorting pencils," I said with a nod. I sounded very wise and experienced.

Dad took the bottle of taco sauce and drizzled some over his dinner. "Nobody starts at the top, kid."

Except superheroes, I thought, hiding a smile behind my taco. And it's true. Even the smallest superhero duty is a big deal. I supposed I should be glad that my nonsuper job for the next two weeks was going to be a low-stress one.

"And sooner or later," Mom said with a sigh, "we all feel like we're just chained to our desk."

"Speaking of being chained to a desk," said Dad, "would you like to hear about Howie's first day on the job?"

I gulped down the bite of taco I'd just taken. "Howie got chained to a desk?"

"Well, handcuffed, to be precise," Dad said, chuckling.

"TELL ME!"

"Well, it was lunchtime when Howie and I got to the station house, so there weren't too many detectives around. Anyway, one of the uniform cops, Ted Morrison, came down to our

43

department to consult on a case. Of course, he had his sidearm and his cuffs with him, and Howie was pretty fascinated. He was staring at Morrison as though he were some kind of *superhero*."

I let out a loud choke of laughter.

"Morrison offered to show Howie the cuffs. One minute Howie was just holding them, and the next he'd somehow managed to cuff himself to the bottom drawer of the chief's desk."

"My goodness," said Mom, filling a second taco for me and handing it across the table. "Poor Howie!"

"Oh, it gets better," said Dad, smiling. "At this point, Ted and I still hadn't noticed what Howie had done. And Howie was too embarrassed to ask for the key, so he quietly opened the chief's top drawer, took out a paper clip, and tried to pick the lock on the handcuffs."

"Let me guess," I said. "The paper clip broke in the lock and jammed it."

"Right! How did you know?"

I rolled my eyes. "Dad, I've known the kid for ten years. Trust me, that is *such* a Howie thing to do!" It wasn't that I didn't feel any sympathy for Howie—I did. But after being friends with a boy like Howie for so long, the goofy things that happen to him don't surprise you so much anymore.

"Poor Howie," said Mom again.

"The worst part," Dad continued, "was that the chief keeps his lunch in the bottom drawer, but with Howie hooked to the handle, there was no way for the chief to get to his pastrami on rye. It took three detectives and a janitor with a hacksaw to finally solve the problem." Dad was trying to keep from laughing as he finished the story.

"Howie must have felt awful," said Mom.

44

"He did at first," said Dad. "But it turns out that back when Morrison was a rookie, he had a handcuff mishap his first day on the job. Cuffed himself to the steering wheel of a squad car, I think it was."

I'd finished my second taco and was reaching for a third shell.

"Looks like you worked up an appetite with all that pencil sorting," Mom observed.

"I guess I did," I said, heaping olives and jalapeño peppers into the shell. "And you know something? I can't wait to do it again tomorrow!"

☆

I locked my bedroom door.

I never had to do that before I became a superhero, but I couldn't take a chance on Mom or Dad popping in to say goodnight while I was flipping through the scrapbook.

I plunked the large album in front of me on my bed and opened it. On the first page was an inscription in gold ink:

> To All Who Have Been
> Born and Who Shall Be
> Born of the Mighty Pie
> Ancestry, Herein Is Writ
> Your Proud History

Cool. I'd never read anything with the word *writ* in it before!

Feeling curious and important, I turned the page and found an elaborate diagram: the Zip family tree.

I studied it for several minutes, suddenly ravenous for information about my Super roots. I already knew that my grandpa Zack's grandmother, Zelda (also known, according to a notation in the diagram, as Hero Zephyr), was a superhero. Zelda's uncle Zeke (aka Hero Zinger) was a hero, as was her cousin Zita. Some of my relatives had married into other Super clans; others, like Grandpa, had married Ordinaries.

I scanned the page until I came to the place where Grandpa had carefully filled in my name—Zoe Alexandra Richards—and the year of my birth. By counting upward through the branches of the tree, I determined that I was a seventh-generation hero.

And so was Zander.

My breath caught in my throat as I slid my finger across the page and saw that, although no one had ever so much as mentioned it before, I actually had a distant cousin who was twelve years old like me.

His name was Alexander Richards, but he was called Zander. (Apparently my family takes the whole *Z* thing very seriously.) I wondered why Grandpa Zack hadn't mentioned Zander to me. I kind of liked knowing I had a cousin my own age out there somewhere who was going through the same weird and wonderful experience I was. I made a mental note to ask Grandpa about it as soon as he and Gran returned from vacation. But Zander, being a "Gen 7" like me, was part of the Zip present, and this paper I had to write was supposed to be about the past, so I figured I could leave my questions about this Zander kid for a later date and turned the page.

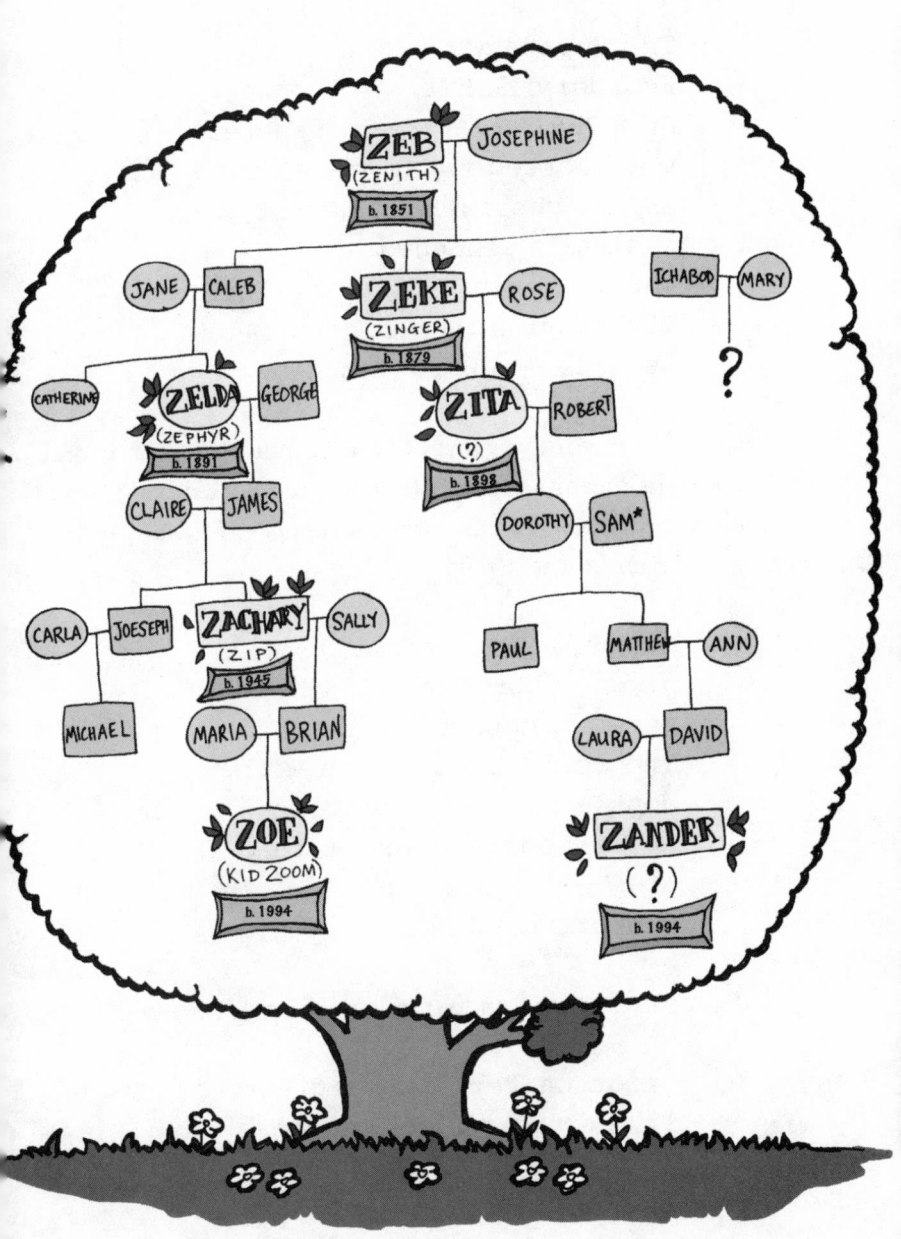

<u>The Supernews</u>
February 13, 1964
SWEETBRIAR—A great disaster
was averted today when Hero
Zip successfully disarmed
a missile launched by
supervillain N-Cina-Ray-Tor.
The mission was originally
assigned to Hero Gumption.

Gumption? The word was sort of familiar, but I had to stop and think about its meaning. Then I remembered—we'd had it on a vocabulary test a few weeks earlier. *Gumption: boldness; spunk; guts.* I went back to the article.

Gumption was recently
given control of our latest
interatmospheric aircraft.
The craft is outfitted with
double-intensified turbo
power-boosters and state-
of-the-art stealth
capabilities.

That last part sounded oddly familiar. I kept on reading:

Unfortunately, as the craft
lifted off, a flock of geese
flew directly into the
flight path. Gumption was

48

forced to land the
craft before reaching
cruising altitude. Luckily,
Gumption's current trainee,
Apprentice Hero Maximus,
exhibited good
judgment and quick thinking
and contacted Zip, thus
turning the mission over to
him. Acting with customary
bravery and speed, Zip was
able to halt the missile's
progress and deflect it into
outer space. At present,
N-Cina-Ray-Tor remains at
large, but Zip will continue
his pursuit of the criminal.
This valiant achievement
marks Zip's forty-ninth
rescue this year, which gives
him a career total of 1,784
successful missions, the
highest tally of all time!

I flipped to the next page and was not surprised to see a news clipping that included a photo of Zip apprehending N-Cina-Ray-Tor. The arrest, according to the headline, took place only one day after my grandpa had saved the earth from this bad guy's missile.

Filled with pride, I closed the book. Maybe writing this essay wouldn't be such a drag after all. It might be fun—not to mention informative—to learn about my legacy. And I'd already learned one extremely cool thing: not only is my grandfather Sweetbriar's premier dry cleaner, he was also one awesome superhero in his day!

CHAPTER

7

THE rest of the week went smoothly, if uneventfully. I reported for work at Electra's and was given loads of jobs to do, like stacking paper and making sure she had enough pencils in each color. She'd sit at her desk and draw and write and tell me things about ink quality and printer deadlines while I checked her ideas against old issues to be sure the action was consistent. I even caught a mistake—she was drawing one of Lightning Girl's archenemies, the glamorous Claw-dette, with red polished claws, but when the previous episode had ended, Claw-dette had just gotten a French manicure.

Mornings at school were hectic. It felt as if the teachers were trying to squeeze in as many classes as they could before our early departure. Everything seemed to be moving at top speed—which wasn't such a big deal for me, of course. On Friday morning, Emily and I blew past each other in the hallway.

"Hi," I said, rushing toward my locker while several other sixth graders hurried by.

"Hi." She was practically jogging in the direction of the science lab. "Hey, let's meet at the Burger Barn for lunch today, after school, before work-study."

"Sounds good."

"Invite Howie and Josh, too. I'll ask Caitlin."

"Okay."

"See ya," she called, disappearing around the corner.

I opened my locker, searching for my history book. Mr. Diaz poked his head out of his classroom and smiled at me. "Time's a-wasting, Zoe," he joked. "Pick up the pace! Can't you go any faster?"

I pulled out my history book and smiled back at him. "I'll try," I said. But inside I was laughing. *If you only knew, Mr. Diaz. If you only knew!*

I was the first one to get to the Burger Barn after school. Guess how!

Okay, so it was risky using my superspeed in broad daylight, but it had been a while since I'd cut loose, and I really needed to flex my supermuscles! I couldn't afford to get rusty, could I? I was careful to keep to the quieter roads and woodsy lots to avoid being seen.

When Emily arrived, I noticed that she was wearing one of the great outfits I'd helped pick out for her—a little plaid skirt in hot pink and lime green with a green crocheted shrug over a white T-shirt. We'd been in such a rush when I'd seen her at school that it hadn't registered. She really did look like a magazine editor! I, on the other hand, was wearing old blue jeans and a sweatshirt with a tear in the elbow. Emily slid into the booth and eyed my getup.

"So I guess Electra Allbright prefers a casual work environment, huh?"

"I'm going to be scrubbing out ink bottles this afternoon," I explained. "You look great. What's on your work schedule for the day?"

Her eyes were sparkling with excitement. "I'm going to be sitting in on a big meeting. Harriet—she's my mentor—is interviewing Rachel Anne Donovan. *Rachel Anne Donovan!* Can you believe it?"

I had to think for a minute to remember who exactly Rachel Anne Donovan was. I knew I'd heard her name from Emily a million times, and if she was being interviewed by *Go, Girl!* she was most likely some big shot in the fashion industry—I just couldn't recall exactly what she was famous for. Was she a supermodel? A makeup artist? An A-list photographer?

"Who's Rachel Anne Donovan?" asked Josh, who was just joining us in the booth. I silently thanked him for asking the question so I didn't have to.

"She's only the most awesome handbag designer on the whole entire planet!" Emily gushed.

Now I remembered. R.A.D. BAGS—that was Rachel Anne Donovan's brand name. Emily thought they're just too chic for words and had been begging her parents for months to buy her one, but even the smallest bag in the R.A.D. line cost major bucks. Mrs. Huang had told Emily that she wasn't about to shell out two hundred and eighty dollars for a purse that was only big enough to hold two tissues and a tube of lip gloss. I had to admit, I couldn't blame her.

Josh took a seat beside me in the booth. "That's great, Em."

"Thanks. And guess what else! The editors are even thinking of letting me write a fashion-for-middle-schoolers column when the project is over, kind of a 'preteen at large' contributing editor gig."

I reached across the table to give her a high five. "Cool-litzer, here we come!"

Then I turned to Josh. "How's your job going?" I asked him.

"It's awesome. I'm doing lots of hands-on work with endangered insects."

"That's gross," said Caitlin, sidling up to the table, then softening her snippy comment with a broad smile. "Hi, everybody!"

Howie was right behind her, looking as though he had something terribly important on his mind. "Hey, guys."

Caitlin sat down beside Emily, and Howie squeezed into the booth next to Josh, which meant Josh had to scoot down closer to me so that our shoulders touched. The waitress came and we all ordered burgers and sodas.

"How's police work, Howie?" Emily asked.

"EXCITING."

We all waited for him to elaborate, but after a few moments, it became clear that he wasn't going to. I figured Howie thought his work required top-secret classification.

"How's the comic-book world?" Caitlin asked me when the waitress was gone. "Do you have to bring your own crayons, or does Electra Allbright let you use hers? Oh, let me guess—

you've got a big lunch meeting with Superman, Spider-Man and the Incredible Hulk tomorrow?"

Josh grinned at me. "Now, that's what I'd call a *power* lunch."

"The comic-book world rocks! I'm learning a ton of fascinating stuff," I told Caitlin firmly. "How's your job?"

Caitlin's cool expression vanished and she looked away. "Fine," she said.

Howie raised his eyebrows, and I could tell he knew something about Caitlin's job at the florist. The waitress returned and handed out our sodas, and there was a moment of confusion when Emily was given Josh's root beer by mistake. Caitlin looked glad of the distraction, but Howie wasn't about to let the topic drop.

"Aren't you going to tell them what happened?" he prompted.

Caitlin shot him a look that could have frozen the soda in his glass. "Of course I am," she said. "Why wouldn't I? After all, it was just an honest mistake. It was kind of amusing, actually."

"Hmmm." Howie took a long sip of his cola. "I don't think Mr. Adamson thought it was amusing."

"What mistake?" Emily asked. "Who's Mr. Adamson?"

Caitlin let out a long sigh, then forced a bright smile. "The Adamsons are regular customers at the flower shop. Yesterday, Mr. Adamson called and ordered an elaborate bouquet and asked that it be sent to his wife, with a card that said, 'I love you more each day, Hugs and kisses, Melvin.' Well, I took the order and prepared the arrangement and had it delivered to Mrs. Adamson."

"So what was the problem?" Josh asked.

"The problem," said Howie, "was that the phone call wasn't from Mr. Michael Adamson, it was from Mr. Melvin *Abram*son. So when Mr. Adamson got home and saw the mushy card his

55

wife had gotten from some guy named Melvin, he was furious. He thought his wife was dating another man!"

I gulped. Caitlin was studying the tabletop. She looked uncomfortable, but not especially sorry. In fact, she looked as if she was trying not to crack up.

"So what happened?" Emily asked.

Howie shook his head. "It was awful. Mrs. Adamson swore she didn't know anyone named Melvin, but Mr. Adamson said the flowers were proof that she was lying. Finally, they had to call my grandpa to get to the bottom of the mess. He figured out that Caitlin had gotten the names confused and sent the arrangement to the wrong wife. But to make matters worse, Mr. Abramson called to say that he was in the doghouse because his wife never received her birthday bouquet."

"Adamson, Abramson," Caitlin said offhandedly. "It could have happened to anyone."

Sure it could, I thought. Except it had happened to *her*, and there was something about Caitlin Abbott that made me the teensiest bit suspicious. . . .

The waitress arrived with our burgers and we dug in, eating quickly because no one wanted to be late to work.

Especially me. Washing bottles may not sound like fancy work, but it was cool by me. I'd scrub at the sink in the workroom, and Electra would draw, and I'd get to hear more of her stories from the comics-writing world. For the world's biggest Electra Allbright fan (that's me, by the way), what could be better?

When I arrived at Electra's mansion, I found that she had left

56

the front door unlocked for me. I let myself in and headed up to her attic studio, my backpack stuffed with Grandpa's huge scrapbook—thudding against my shoulder.

I entered the attic and found Electra frowning at a storyboard.

"Hi," I said from the doorway.

"Hello, Zoe," said Electra, not looking up. "Hope you didn't mind seeing yourself up—I'm experiencing a comic-book author's worst nightmare at the moment."

"What's that?" I inquired.

Electra let out an exasperated huff. "Writer's block." She frowned at the sketches in front of her, then glanced up at me with a grin. "I could use some input."

I put my backpack on the floor beside the door and crossed the attic to her table. "Here's the problem," she said. "Lightning Girl has been captured by the villain Riptide. Nasty guy . . ."

I nodded. "I remember him. He's the one who trained the killer sharks to breathe on land and set them loose in shopping malls all over America."

"Right. Well, now he and Lightning Girl have crossed paths again and he's just sealed her into an airtight room. No windows, no vents, and the door is padlocked on the outside, so she can't fire a lightning bolt at it."

"YIKES."

"Indeed." Electra tapped her pencil on the last two empty squares in the long sequence. "Riptide is filling the room with water. See? It's up to LG's knees already. But now that I've got her stuck in the room with the water gushing in . . . well, frankly, I'm having a hard time coming up with a solution to get her out."

I could feel my heart racing with excitement, because (a) I'm such a big Lightning Girl fan and this is exactly the kind of suspense I live for, and (b) Electra was seriously asking for my input! She needed *my* help to figure out a way to rescue our hero!

"Any thoughts?" she asked, sounding a bit desperate.

"Well . . ." I studied the pencil sketches of Lightning Girl in her hero outfit that looked so much like mine, with the zippers and the hooks, and the supercool insignia, and the tool belt and . . .

"THE CAPE!"

Electra gave me a look that said "Go on," so I did.

"It's got to be a new one—you'll have to go back and add a scene. Is that okay?"

"Of course. . . . Keep talking. . . ."

"Well, I know because I've read every Lightning Girl ever written that her cape is just made of your basic, ordinary indestructible fabric. But let's say somewhere in this book she decides she needs a more aerodynamic cape, and maybe a new color . . . how about here?" I pointed to a place near the beginning of the story.

"All right." Electra made a notation on the storyboard. "And . . . ?"

"And while she's at it, she asks the suit designer to upgrade the cape a little, give it some high-tech properties, like superabsorbency, which she knows has become all the rage among trendy superheroes. And the designer says, 'Sure, I just got some superabsorbent fabric the other day, and the color would be divine on you.'"

58

"Yes!" Electra cried. "Yes, and if we put this scene in early enough, by the time Lightning Girl heads off on her mission to fight Riptide, she'll already have the new cape."

"So when she's stuck in the room and the water starts gushing in, she can use the cape to sop it all up and save herself."

"Wonderful!" said Electra, scribbling the image into the two empty blocks. "Zoe, this is brilliant. Frankly, I can't believe I forgot about superabsorbent capes—" She stopped short, her pencil pausing for just a second before it began moving again. "I

mean, I can't believe I hadn't *thought of* superabsorbent fabric. How lucky for me that you're so inventive!"

I smiled. "It just sort of came to me," I fibbed. Of course, the fact of the matter was that I just happen to have a super-absorbent cape of my own, and it just happened to be stowed across the room in my backpack . . .

. . . which, just at that moment, started to make a whirring sound.

My backpack was *whirring?*

Well, that was new.

I thought I saw Electra's pencil pause again. I swallowed hard, expecting her to ask what the noise was and where it was coming from. But she didn't say a word; in fact, maybe she hadn't paused at all—maybe I'd only imagined it. She seemed to be so into her sketches of the cape that she didn't even hear the whir.

"Uh . . . excuse me," I said, and hurried back toward the door-way.

I grabbed my backpack and ran down the stairs with it, then ducked into the second-floor bathroom and closed the door.

Okay . . . now what? Something was whirring, but I couldn't tell what or where it was. I checked the front pocket of my pack, then the main one. I ran my hands along the straps and even fid-dled with the key chains, which I already knew were just plain key chains.

Finally, I pulled out my supersuit and checked the tool belt. There, clipped to the left section, was what looked like a minia-ture walkie-talkie. I removed it from the belt and pushed the tiny green button that said Talk.

"Zoe speaking," I said; then, to sound official, I added, "I mean, Kid Zoom here."

"Well, hello there!" came a pleasant male voice. It was one of those twangy nasal voices that people often associate with old-time telephone operators. For a minute, I thought maybe it was a joke.

"To whom am I speaking?" I asked.

"This is Thatcher."

"Thatcher who?"

"I am only authorized to introduce myself as Thatcher," the voice informed me cheerfully. "Sorry, but rules are rules."

"Um . . . how did you get this number?"

"Well, technically, it's not a number, it's a wavelength, but that's not important now. I am a dispatcher at the Superhero Federation's central communications hub."

So I was talking to Thatcher the Dispatcher? Oh, brother.

"What can I do for you?" I asked, still not sure why this guy was contacting me.

"Well, I haven't had my lunch, so if you wouldn't mind picking up a pepperoni and anchovy pizza and speeding it over here, I'd be very grateful."

I frowned. "You want me to bring you a pizza?"

At that, Thatcher cracked up. "Only kidding, Zoom. That was just a little dispatcher humor."

"Oh."

"Actually, I'm sending you on a mission."

"Really? When?"

"Now."

"Now?"

"Yes, now. Right now."

A million thoughts hit me at once. I was about to go on my first mission without Grandpa Zack anywhere around to help. It

61

was exciting, it was terrifying, it was . . . *really bad timing!* What was I supposed to tell Electra? And what if she came downstairs and heard me talking to Thatcher?

"Zoom?"

"I'm here. What's the mission?"

"There's a cat stuck in a tree."

I blinked. "Excuse me?"

"I said there is a cat stuck in a tree and you are being dispatched to rectify the situation immediately, if not sooner."

What was sooner than immediately? I wondered. And wasn't this a job for the volunteer fire department?

"You're kidding."

"Nope."

Well, I'd been hoping for something big, and boy, was this *not* it! But I was a superhero, and I was bound by Federation rules to undertake any and all missions assigned to me. Even the stupid ones.

"Fine," I grumbled, pulling the rest of my Super getup out of the backpack. "So where exactly is this tree with the cat stuck in it?"

"Would you prefer latitude and longitude or the address?"

Well, since I'm not Christopher Columbus . . . "The address, please."

"Forty-seven-thirty-six Applegate Boulevard, Sweetbriar."

"Got it."

"Proceed with caution, Zoom."

"Thanks, Thatcher."

I returned the communication device to my tool belt, stuffed it into the backpack, and went back to the studio.

Electra was bent over the storyboard, finishing up the super-absorbent cape.

"I have to go," I blurted out; then, remembering that this was not a friendly visit but an actual job, I said, "I mean, would it be all right if I left early today?"

Electra looked up from her drawing, concern in her eyes. "Is anything wrong?"

Well, there's a cat stuck in a tree, I thought wryly. "No. It's just that I remembered something. I have a dentist appointment today. My mom made it way before we knew about the work-study program, and I forgot to tell Mr. Diaz about it. And, well, it's one of those big-deal appointments—something to do with my molars, I think. Or was it my wisdom teeth? Well, either way, it has to do with the really important teeth, not just the regular ones, so it would be kind of a problem if I missed it."

I thought I saw a smile tugging at the corner of Electra's mouth.

"Of course, I know it's also kind of a problem to leave work early, and some bosses might get really mad and fire a person, even if their molars *were* in danger. . . ."

Electra held up a hand to stop me. "Go," she said with a smile. "Believe me, I understand about . . . molars. More than you know."

I turned and hurried out of the room, taking both sets of stairs two at a time. On the main level of the house, I ducked into the powder room and was in my supersuit within seconds. On the front porch, I paused to get my bearings, deciding on the best and most discreet route to forty-seven-thirty-six Applegate Boulevard. Then I took a deep breath and got ready for some serious superspeed.

"Kitty-cat, here I come!"

63

CHAPTER 8

THE *Zoo?*

I skidded to a superhalt at the tall iron gates and saw that yes, the address given to me by Thatcher the Dispatcher was for the Sweetbriar Zoo. Weird.

The communication device on my tool belt began to whir again; I snatched it from its clip and spoke into the mouthpiece.

"Thatcher?"

"Who else?" said Thatcher. "Have you reached your destination?"

"I've reached the zoo," I answered.

"Well done."

"So I'm *supposed* to be at the zoo?"

"Yes, and there isn't much time to spare. Move it. Go to the far west corner."

I sped through the zoo. Luckily it was lunchtime, which meant nearly all the zoo visitors would be crowded around the penguin pool to enjoy feeding session. When I was a kid, that was always my favorite part of coming to the Sweetbriar Zoo. Unfortunately, the penguins' antics rarely lasted more than half an hour, so I wouldn't have the place to myself for long.

I zoomed on.

It was a pretty little zoo, with lots of shrubs and trees planted around the grounds. The animals in their pits and cages all looked well fed, clean, and content. But wasn't this a pretty strange place for a pet cat to be stuck in a tree?

I reached the far west corner and stopped dead. Yup, there was a cat stuck in a tree.

Only it wasn't a regular domestic kitty-cat, the sort of cat you'd call the fire department to rescue.

Oh, no. This was a bigger cat than that. A *much* bigger cat. A *tiger*, to be precise. It was Cleo, one of the Sweetbriar Zoo's star attractions. She was big, beautiful, and very fierce looking.

And she wasn't alone. There was a little boy up there with her, and she was creeping along the branch toward him!

I took a second to assess the situation. For safety, the tigers lived in a deep, wide area below the main level of the zoo. The pit was planted to look like a jungle habitat, with trees and boulders and a small pool. Visitors viewed the tigers by looking down through a tall fence. The tree that the boy had climbed was a giant old oak, which grew just outside the fence around the pit.

There was a balloon caught in the high branches of the tree, so I figured that the kid, who looked about four years old, had climbed the tree to retrieve it. The problem was that the oak tree's branches had grown over the fence and reached out and over the tiger pit. The other problem was that one of the trees planted inside the pit had grown tall enough so that its uppermost branches reached the lowest branches of the overgrown tree.

Cleo must have noticed the boy and climbed the tree in the pit to reach him.

And now there they were, tiger and child, perched on a fat branch above the tiger pit, while two tiger cubs and another huge tiger—Cleo's mate, I guessed—watched from below.

I took a superleap into the tree, landing easily between the boy and the tiger with my back to the boy.

"Are you a superhero?" said a trembling voice behind me.

"Yup," I said without taking my eyes off the tiger. Now I knew why they were called *big* cats. Close up, it was huge, with thick glossy fur, gleaming amber eyes, and neat round ears that were focused on nothing but *me*.

The tiger let out a low growl, curling its top lip to reveal long, curved, razor-sharp teeth. My heart thudded, and I wondered if my supersuit could withstand tiger claws.

"I wanna get down!" the boy wailed suddenly. "I wanna get down *now!*"

If I hadn't been so hypnotized by the tiger's eyes, I might have turned around and stopped the boy from doing what he did next . . . which was to fling himself at me, wrapping his arms around my neck, clinging for dear life.

"Can you fly?" he sobbed damply into my ear.

"Um, no," I answered as the tiger crept closer. "But I can jump." Clutching the child and holding my breath, I leaped off the branch.

"WHEEEEEE!" he cried. Clearly, the thrill of a superleap outweighed the terror of facing death by tiger.

66

I landed easily on the grassy area outside the fence of the tiger pit and managed to detach the boy from my neck. The tiger was watching us from the other side of the fence, lashing her tail in frustration. I held her gaze, determined not to let her know how much she'd scared me. She let out a huge roar, then turned and sprang gracefully back into the pit to join her family.

"Wait here," I told the kid, then went over to the tree and braced my hands against the broad trunk. Summoning all my superstrength, I pushed the giant tree as hard as I could. It moved several feet away from the pit, dragging its deep roots with it. As I pushed, the tree left a wake of earth and pavement, but I didn't care. That could be fixed. I just didn't want to give Cleo a chance to climb that tree again and escape.

When the tree and all its overhanging branches were a safe distance from the trees in the pit, I went back to the little boy.

"That was fun," he said.

"No, it wasn't!" I corrected him, in a voice I hoped was kind but firm. I was trying to model myself on old episodes of *Wonder Woman*. "That was a very dangerous thing to do. You should never have climbed that tree."

He shrugged, as if all he could remember was leaping through the air.

I began to feel a shred of sympathy for parents. "Promise me you'll never do that again."

"Okay, I promise."

"Where's your mommy?"

"Watching the penguins. I snuck away. I like tigers better." He looked me up and down. "You're not Superman, are you? What's your name?"

I bit my lip. "I can't tell you."

He pouted. "That stinks."

"Yeah. Um . . . listen . . . I'd really appreciate it if you didn't tell anyone I was here, okay? I'll get in major, big-time trouble if you do. You don't want that to happen, do you?"

The little boy shook his head hard. "No way. You saved my life. Even if you did forget my balloon . . ."

I heard voices approaching. "Yeah, sorry about that. Wanna see something cool?" I asked.

The boy nodded.

"Okay . . . watch."

I took off at superspeed, and over the sound of the wind in my ears I could hear the kid gasp with amazement. I knew he'd get a kick out of the blur thing.

I ducked behind a trash can on the opposite side of the tiger pit just as the boy's mom raced up.

"Joey!" she cried, catching him in a hug. "There you are! Why did you run away from the penguin pool?"

"Sorry, Mommy," he said. "I just wanted a closer look at the tigers."

Well, he sure got it, didn't he? I thought. And that cat wasn't the only thing he got a good look at—he'd seen Kid Zoom up close into the bargain. I could only hope the boy would keep his promise and not tell anyone about his brush with a super-hero. I was pretty sure that even if he did crack and tell the grown-ups

who'd saved him, they'd just chalk it up to an overactive imagination. I decided there was no point in worrying about something I couldn't control.

I peeked around the trash can and saw that a zookeeper was staring at the "transplanted" tree in shock. Maybe he'd figure it was the work of a mini-earthquake or something. But I couldn't worry about that, either. It was done. I'd been careful not to be spotted. And the important thing was that the little boy was safe.

All I wanted to do now was find a secluded place, like maybe behind the reptile house, and change out of my . . .

UH-OH.

My backpack was still at Electra's house. I'd left it in the downstairs powder room with all my normal clothes and my schoolbooks and . . .

. . . Grandpa's scrapbook!

How could I have done something so irresponsible? How could I have been so careless? Grandpa had warned me that it would be big trouble if that scrapbook fell into the wrong hands—heck, into *any* hands other than my own.

I needed to get my backpack, and fast. Luckily, being fast is my thing.

First, I'd zoom home and get into my room by jumping through the window, so as not to run into Mom or Dad on my way through the house. I'd change my clothes, hide my suit at the back of my closet, then leap out the window and superspeed my way back to Electra's.

As I raced around the outskirts of Sweetbriar, I told myself that

she probably hadn't even noticed the backpack yet; she'd probably been so involved in the absorbent-cape story line that she
hadn't gone downstairs. And even if she had, what were the
chances of her using the powder room? The house was huge. It
had, like, a zillion bathrooms. Why would she trudge all the way
down to the tiny powder room?

I was in my backyard in seconds, and with an effortless bounce,
I was on the windowsill and scooting into my bedroom.

Suit off. Clothes on. Fast, fast, fast.

And now all I had to do was get back to Electra's place before
she found the backpack.

I was two steps from the window when I heard the voices
downstairs.

And realized I was too late.

CHAPTER

9

I crept down the stairs and peered into the kitchen. There at the table, drinking tea and munching on banana chocolate chip muffins, were Mom and Electra. They seemed to be chatting away like old friends. I could see my backpack propped in the corner by the refrigerator. Well, at least that would save me a trip to Electra's mansion. But what if Electra mentioned my molars to Mom? Mom knew I didn't have a dentist appointment. She'd want to know why I cut out of work and, more importantly, where I'd been all this time.

I forced myself to put a calm expression on my face and stepped into the kitchen.

"HI."

Both women looked up at me and smiled.

72

"Hello, slowpoke," said Mom.

Slowpoke? Now, *that* was funny—although Mom didn't know it.

"What do you mean?" I asked, trying to sound casual.

"Well, Ms. Allbright said she sent you home early today, but later she realized you forgot your schoolbag, so she brought it here. What took you so long to get home?"

She didn't sound mad, or even worried (which surprised me, because my mom worries about me whenever I'm out of her sight for more than three seconds). She just sounded curious.

"Oh, well, I, uh—well, halfway home I realized I didn't have my backpack, so I went all the way back to Burger Barn to see if I'd left it there. Then I went back to Elec—um, Ms. Allbright's house, but I guess she was on her way here." I shrugged, praying that Electra hadn't said anything about a dentist appointment. "Then I came home."

I had to stop myself from hopping over the kitchen table and checking my backpack to see if I could tell whether Electra had looked inside. "Thank you for bringing it over."

Electra gave a little wave. "It was nothing."

A buzzer sounded in the laundry room, and Mom stood up. "Dryer's done," she said. "Will you excuse me for one sec? If I don't take Brian's shirts out right away, they'll be wrinkled beyond recognition." She turned toward the laundry room, calling over her shoulder, "Zoe, why don't you pour Ms. Allbright another cup of tea? And have a muffin—I just made them."

"Sure."

I went to the stove and got the teapot. Electra held her cup out and I poured, then returned the pot to the stove.

"I figured I'd better bring that backpack over," she said as the

73

steam wafted up from the cup, "what with all the top-secret data inside."

Her words hit me like a truck. "Top- . . . secret . . . data . . . ?"

"You know . . . all that Josh-and-Zoe stuff on your notebook. I didn't think you'd want that information falling into the wrong hands."

I let out a huge sigh of relief. "Right. Yes. Josh and Zoe. Top-secret."

"Hey," said Electra, smiling at me over the rim of her teacup. "I was in sixth grade myself once, you know."

She took a sip of tea as Mom returned from the laundry room carrying a pile of Dad's folded shirts.

"I have an idea for a comic book," Mom joked. "A superhero who flies around matching socks and ironing shirts. You can call her Laundry Girl!"

Electra laughed. "I bet it would be a big seller," she said, standing. "Well, I'd better be going. Thank you for the tea and muffins, Mrs. Richards. Simply delish!"

"You're welcome. And thank you for bringing Zoe's schoolbag."

"Well, it wouldn't do to have my apprentice missing any homework, now, would it?" Electra picked up her purse and slung it over her shoulder.

"Hey, that's a R.A.D. BAG," I said. "My friend Emily is meeting the designer today."

"It's gorgeous," said Mom.

"It's overpriced is what it is," said Electra, sounding a bit embarrassed. "It was a gift from my publisher. Honestly, I would never have bought one of these ridiculously expensive things for myself."

"I agree," said Mom. "But the kids are mad for them. Miss

74

Bettancourt just created a big, flashy display of the various R.A.D. BAG styles in her boutique window."

Miss Bettancourt is a sweet old lady who owns a small boutique on Main Street. She carries all the newest styles and trends, even though she herself dresses in dainty, old-fashioned dresses and sensible shoes. Emily has always found that contrast amusing.

Electra turned to me. "So . . . you have a wonderful weekend, and I'll see you on Monday."

The minute she stepped out the door, I grabbed my backpack and dashed up to my room to check the scrapbook.

It seemed to be exactly as I'd left it, bookmarks in all the right pages and notes where I'd stuck them.

Everything was fine. The scrapbook was untouched; Electra hadn't ratted me out about the phony dentist appointment (although I still wasn't sure why—she must have known I'd lied from the way Mom didn't mention it); even the little boy from the zoo was probably safe at home right this very minute, dreaming about tigers and superheroes.

But it all could just as easily have gone wrong.

Suddenly, I was exhausted. Tired to the very marrow of my superbones. I sank down on my bed, trying not to let my mind wander to all the disasters that might have occurred in the course of this one day. Stress, worry, anxiety . . . each feeling, each thought, sent a shiver along my spine.

I put my head on my pillow and closed my eyes. Sheesh, this was one day I didn't want to live over.

On Saturday, I finished my essay on my Zip ancestry. I sent my report (of which I was quite proud) to the Superhero Federation via e-mail, then brought the scrapbook back to Grandpa's garage for safekeeping.

And then . . . I practiced.

Grandpa's backyard is where this whole Super experience started, so it seemed like a logical place to get in some much-needed review. I was safely hidden by the tall fence that enclosed the yard and free to completely cut loose.

I started out by running laps. I circled the yard a thousand times in one minute. Not bad. Then I worked on my superefficient stopping technique by sprinting fifty yards, then digging my heels into the ground and coming to a full stop, an instant halt.

The first time I stopped like that, I got a little woozy, but I shook it off and tried again. The second time, I left a pretty sizable divot in Grandpa's lawn (I was sure he'd understand, though). The third time, I did it perfectly. From ninety miles an hour to zero without even a wobble.

I finished up with a few thousand sit-ups.

After that, I ran a comb through my hair and went to meet Emily at the megaplex. Fifteen high-def surround-sound theaters in one building.

She was waiting for me at the candy counter. She'd already ordered me a medium popcorn (the container was practically the size of a bathtub!) and a king-sized box of chocolate-covered raisins. She got her usual: black licorice and a large blue-raspberry slush.

We were making our way toward theater number twelve when someone called, "Hi, Zoe. Hi, Emily."

I wasn't surprised to see Megan Talbot and her crowd right

behind us. They were eighth graders; coming to the megaplex was pretty much a standard weekend activity for them. They didn't really care which movie they saw. They just wanted to be seen by other eighth graders.

"Look," Emily whispered as the girls approached. "They've all got R.A.D. BAGS!"

She was right—the outrageous designs were unmistakable. Each of the four eighth graders was carrying a different style. I did some quick calculations and determined that we were looking at roughly fifteen hundred dollars' worth of accessories.

Ridiculous!

"I love your purse," Emily said to Megan.

"Thanks," said Megan, then added, "It's a R.A.D. BAG. Have you heard of them?"

"Heard of them?" I said. "Emily interviewed Rachel Anne Donovan yesterday."

Emily blushed as the eighth graders made a fuss over this news.

"What was she like?"

"Very cool. And nice."

"What kind of things did she talk about?"

"My mentor, Harriet, asked Rachel why her bags cost so much," Emily explained. "At first I thought that was sort of a rude question, but Rachel was actually happy to answer it. She told us that she's really into environmentalism and animal rights, so she only uses faux leather and fur. Ordinarily, faux materials cost less, but Rachel insists on extremely high-quality stuff, which is why the products look and feel real. It costs her extra money, not to mention time, to make her handbags without harming animals. And

77

her manufacturing process actually exceeds all the government's environmental standards. That's why she has to charge higher prices."

I hadn't known that. I wondered if my mom would think differently about spending all that money on a purse if she knew it came with a conscience.

"Well, to tell you the truth," said Megan, "we didn't pay all that much for these bags. We got them at Miss Bettancourt's boutique. She's selling them for seventy percent off the suggested retail price. They were actually very reasonable."

I'd have to mention it to my mother. Maybe she'd want one after all if she could get it at such a bargain price.

Then one of the girls noticed that the movie was about to start, so they said good-bye and hurried off to get good seats.

Emily and I continued through the huge megaplex toward theater number twelve.

"I wonder how Miss Bettancourt can afford to sell R.A.D. BAGS at such a discount?" I mused aloud as we took our seats.

But the music was starting and Emily was already transfixed by the first trailer, so I settled into my seat and cracked open my chocolate-covered raisins. The handbags could wait.

CHAPTER 10

ON Monday at school, Mr. Diaz handed out two-page evaluation forms. "Please give these to your mentors today," he said. "The first page is for their comments on last week's work. The second is for this week. There is also an envelope for them to use to send it back to me here at school."

I arrived at Electra's at twelve-thirty, evaluation form in hand, only to find the door open again. I hurried up to the studio, but before I reached the top stair, Electra burst out of the attic, looking flustered.

"Zoe! I'm sorry, but I'm going to have to cancel our time together for today."

"Is something wrong?"

Electra shot a glance over her shoulder, toward the inside of the studio. "No. Actually, I'm in the middle of a real brainstorm.

The ideas are just pouring out of me. I can hardly draw them fast enough."

"Wow, that sounds great," I said, lifting my foot to the next step. "I'd love to watch you. . . ."

"Frankly," said Electra, "I think I'd be better off working alone this afternoon. When I go into a creative frenzy like this, I just get into a zone—I won't be in much of a mood for company."

I was about to say something about learning through observation, but Electra had already dashed back through the attic door. There was nothing left for me to do but turn and go. Then I remembered the evaluation form.

I went back up the stairs and stuck my head in the door, ready to say "excuse me." But my voice froze in my throat. It was as if a comic book had exploded all over the studio. There were storyboards everywhere—on the worktable, propped on easels, tacked to the wall—and each one depicted a different exciting superhero adventure.

Oh, Electra was in a creative frenzy, all right. But none of the adventures I was looking at had been "created."

They'd been stolen.

I couldn't believe my eyes. Lightning Girl's newest adventures were actually some of Zip's oldest ones. Everything, it seemed, from the rescue of the interatmospheric craft to the smoke-filled Kremlin, had been taken right out of Grandpa's scrapbook.

I felt angry, disappointed, betrayed . . . and worried! This was not good. If Electra published these comics, Grandpa Zack's feats would be revealed. That was one huge step toward exposure! And if that happened, it would all be my fault.

I ran down the stairs, out the door, and down the long driveway. At the bottom, hidden by one of the wide brick pillars that flanked the entrance, I opened my backpack, rummaged around for my communication device, and began punching buttons.

"Hello? Thatcher? Are you there?"

A loud beep sounded, followed by a voice—not Thatcher's, but a robotic one. *"Thank you for calling the Superhero Federation. Please listen carefully, as our menu options have changed. If you have a question regarding Super health benefits, please press one. For information regarding the upcoming Super community tag sale, please press two."*

Tag sale? Were they kidding?

"If you are interested in upgrading your security clearance, press three. If you have reason to believe that you or a hero close to you has risked exposure, and for all other inquiries, please stay on the line. The next available operator will be with you in a moment."

"C'mon," I urged through my teeth. "Hurry."

It seemed as if years passed before I finally made my connection.

"Good afternoon. Exposure Hotline. This is—"

"Thatcher? Is that you?"

"Yes."

"It's me, Kid Zoom."

"Well, hi-dee-ho there, Zoomling. Everyone here at the communications hub has been talking about your great work at the zoo the other day. Well done, well done."

"Thanks, but Thatcher, I have a huge problem. I think I may have accidentally let secret information about my Zip ancestry be revealed to a non-Super."

81

There was a long, worrisome silence.

I winced. "That bad, huh?"

"Hard to say." There was another long pause. "Exposure is a serious and often dangerous matter," said Thatcher, his voice sounding way more somber than before. "Irresponsible heroes who allow themselves to be revealed are severely dealt with."

I gulped. "How severely?"

"Depends on which Federation members are called upon to hand down the penalty. Now . . ." There were faint shuffling sounds, as if he was looking for a pen. "Were you seen performing a heroic activity at the time of exposure and are you now surrounded by an angry mob intent on capturing you for the purpose of scientific research?"

"Uh . . . no."

"Good. Then we aren't talking about an imminent threat of discovery. In that case, someone will be contacting you within ten to fourteen business days to obtain more detailed information regarding this potential exposure issue."

"So I might have to wait two weeks before I know if I'm in trouble or not?"

"Don't worry, Zoom," Thatcher assured me. "I doubt there'll be any actual trouble. It's been my experience that when Ordinaries come face to face with a superhero, they are either too narrow-minded or too frightened to allow themselves to believe it. Most of these potential exposure cases blow over. Trust me."

"REALLY?"

"Really."

I smiled, feeling relieved and comforted. "Hey, Thatch," I said.

"Yes, Zoom?"

"Maybe one of these days I *will* bring you that pizza."

I returned the device to my backpack and began walking slowly, thinking about those storyboards that Electra had clearly not wanted me to see. *Now it was obvious why not!*

I had so many questions: Why had she looked through my personal stuff? It wasn't as if she had needed to search the bag for ID, like when you find a lost wallet and want to return it. So what was the point of snooping? And what could she possibly have thought when she saw the scrapbook? Even someone who wrote about superheroes for a living would have to be at least a little bit shocked to learn that superpowered heroes really did exist, not to mention the fact that the one in question, Zip/Zack, happened to be one of her oldest acquaintances.

It was just too much. I felt sad and angry and generally freaked out all at once.

Suddenly, all I wanted to do was go home.

I found Howie waiting for me on the front porch.

"Well, if it isn't Officer Howie Hunt," I said, grinning and throwing a friendly non-Super punch to his shoulder. "What are you doing here? Am I under arrest?"

"I was wondering if you'd help me out with something," said Howie.

"Sure."

"I think Miss Bettancourt's in trouble. It's not her fault, but I think she's been unknowingly conducting business with an underground counterfeiting ring."

For a second or two I just stood there with my mouth hanging open from shock, partly because it was unthinkable that Miss Bettancourt—knowingly or unknowingly—could ever be involved in anything illegal, and partly because I couldn't believe that this was actually Howie speaking. He sounded so official, so professional.

"What do you mean?" I asked at last.

"Have you ever heard of R.A.D. BAGS?"

Hah. It seemed as if over the past few days I'd heard of nothing else. Emily, Electra, Megan and her sidekicks. "What about them?"

"I've been doing some research down at the station house. You know, on the Internet. I found out that thousands of fake R.A.D. BAGS—the police call them knockoffs—have been manufactured and are being sold all over the country. Well, I managed to piece together a pattern, and it looks like maybe they've reached this part of the country. So maybe the ones Miss B has been selling are actually phony. I want to go down there and get a good look at them."

I thought back to what Megan had said about the bags' being seventy percent off. If they were fakes, that would certainly explain the discount—not that I could imagine a sweet old lady like Miss Bettancourt being part of an interstate counterfeiting business. "Howie, I think you might actually be on to something." I filled him in on what I'd heard about R.A.D. BAGS in the last few days—from Emily, Electra, and Megan. "How can I help?"

"Well, I was hoping you'd come downtown with me to check out the boutique. I'd go myself, but I think it would look less suspicious if we went together. You can keep Miss B busy while I look around for evidence."

"I don't know . . . ," I said. "Is my dad okay with this?"

"Um . . . sure. He's completely okay."

"All right. Let's go."

On our way to the store, we decided our cover would be that Howie was shopping for a gift for his mother and I had come along to help him pick out something nice. We arrived at the boutique about twenty minutes before closing time. No one was in the store except Miss Bettancourt.

"Oh, I've had such a busy day!" she exclaimed when we entered. "Those new designer bags are selling like crazy. I guess everyone loves a bargain." She paused to push some strands of silver hair off her forehead. "Now, how can I help you?"

"I need a gift for my mom," Howie stated, as if reading from a script. "I think she'd like one of these cool bags."

"Well, we've sold out of most of the styles," Miss B said. "But as luck would have it, I'm expecting a delivery this evening. The truck should be arriving just after I close up shop. So if you don't see anything you like tonight, you can come back when I open in the morning and have first crack at it." She pointed us toward the selection of R.A.D. BAGS. "You just holler if you have any questions. I'll be in the stockroom, making sure there's room for the new shipment."

Howie and I went over to the display of purses. "What are we looking for, exactly?" I whispered. "How do we tell if it's a real R.A.D. or not?"

"According to my research"—he opened a small pad and scanned some notes—"there are several indicators if it's a fake.

Shoddy stitching, discoloration in certain suedes, mostly the hot pinks and aubergine tones. They fade more quickly than the mushroom and canary colors."

I was impressed.

He quirked an eyebrow. "Er, what's aubergine tone?"

"Dark purple," I replied. I had Electra's pencils to thank for my thorough knowledge of color names. I pushed the thought of Electra out of my mind—I needed to concentrate on what Howie and I were doing.

"Oh. Well, the only surefire way to tell a knockoff from a genuine R.A.D. BAG is by the logo. You see, Rachel Anne Donovan originally used her own handwriting to create the R.A.D. logo. Look. . . ."

He reached into his pocket and pulled out a picture of the R.A.D. logo he'd printed off the Internet. "There's this peculiar little swirl at the top of her *R*."

I squinted at the *R* in the printout. Sure enough, I saw it—it was little, but it was there.

"Now, look at this," said Howie. He showed me a second printout, of what at first glance looked like the same logo. He pointed. "No swirl. Just a standard capital *R*. This is one of the knockoff logos."

I was stunned. "You figured this out all on your own?"

Howie nodded, blushing. "It's just good old-fashioned detective work. Patience, diligence, and a really powerful magnifying glass."

I turned from the creased pages in Howie's hand to the shelf of display bags in Miss B's window. After looking over my shoulder to make sure Miss B wasn't coming back into the store, I reached out and picked up a purple suede bag, what must have been the aubergine tone.

"Go ahead. Check out the logo," Howie said encouragingly.

I squinted at the small script on the purple bag. Sure enough, the *R* was swirl-less.

"OH, NO!" I gasped.

Howie was right. These bags were fakes, made by counterfeiters. Counterfeiters who were on their way here right now with a new shipment! A creepy feeling filled me. I started checking the logos on the other bags. . . . Knockoffs. All of them!

I turned to Howie, my eyes wide. "Miss Bettancourt would never agree to sell fake bags," I said.

Howie nodded. "I know. The bad guys must have her fooled as much as her customers."

"And the delivery—" I stopped short. "Do you think the counterfeiters are going to deliver the bags themselves?"

"I'd guess so," said Howie. "They probably wouldn't trust an ordinary shipping service with their phony goods."

"How are you two doing over there?" Miss B called, returning from the stockroom.

"Er, f-fine," I stammered. "We . . . we like this purple one, but we also like the striped one with the bamboo handles." I lowered my voice to a whisper and said to Howie, "We should call my dad!"

"NO!"

"No?" I glared at him. "Why not?"

Howie looked down at his sneakers. "He . . . well . . . would be kind of surprised to know I was here."

"You said my dad was okay with your looking for evidence,"

I snapped. "But what you meant was that he was okay with it only because he didn't know exactly what you were doing." I threw my hands in the air. "Howie!"

"Listen, Zoe, this means a lot to me. I don't want your dad to think I'm a total goof. It's not just the thing with the handcuffs. Today I spilled the chief's coffee all over some papers. Turns out those papers were a signed confession."

"Uh-oh."

"Yeah. Major uh-oh. I don't want to blow my chances of ever becoming a detective!"

"I can see how much this means to you, Howie, but still—"

"Miss B said the delivery is scheduled for closing time. That's in"—he checked his watch—"five minutes. If we wait for your dad and his officers, we might lose the opportunity to catch these guys."

I let it all sink in. It wasn't as if Howie were here alone—I mean, he did have a superhero with him. I was pretty sure that even if he messed up, I'd be able to run interference. And it was so important to him to prove he wasn't a total klutz. I knew he wasn't, but even though Howie was one of my best friends, I had to admit that sometimes he didn't show what he could really do.

"Here's the plan," I said. "We'll tell Miss B we're coming back tomorrow to check out the new shipment. Then we'll go around back and hide. When the truck comes, we'll wait for the bad guys to bring the first box of not-so-R.A.D. BAGS into the stockroom, and we'll lock them inside. Then I'll call my dad and get him down here fast."

"I like it!" said Howie. "What about Miss B? What if the bad guys break out of the storeroom and take her hostage or something?"

I thought about it, then marched across the shop to where

Miss B was collecting the day's receipts from the register.

"Such a busy day!" she said. "And now I have to go upstairs to my office and record all these sales on the computer." She frowned. "Hang on, I've just remembered that I have to wait for the delivery to arrive before I can get started. It's going to be a long night!"

"I have an idea," I said. "Why don't you let Howie and me help you with the delivery? We can wait for them and tell them where you want the boxes stacked. That way you can go up and get started on those receipts. We'll come and get you if you need to sign anything."

Miss Bettancourt gave me a grateful smile. "You wouldn't mind? That's awfully nice of you."

"Not at all."

"I'll come down later to lock up," she said, gathering her paperwork and heading toward the door that led to the stairs. "You just holler if you need me. You won't have any trouble, I'm sure. Those men have been very sweet and reliable."

Yeah, right, I thought. *They've got you selling their fake stuff. No wonder they're being sweet.*

We watched as she walked through the door; then we listened to her footsteps on the stairs.

"Okay, now what?" said Howie.

I grabbed a piece of sticky-note paper from the counter and dashed off a quick message telling the delivery guys (otherwise known as the criminals!) to come in and leave the boxes. I signed Miss Bettancourt's name.

"We stick this on the back door to the stockroom and wait for these creepy counterfeiters to show up. We'll leave that door unlocked, and they'll come in looking for Miss B. Meanwhile, we'll hide outside, and when they're in the stockroom, we'll lock them in."

"I can read them their rights," Howie boasted. "I memorized the Miranda spiel."

"Sounds good," I said, but I had no intention of letting Howie anywhere near these guys. Counterfeiting was a serious crime, and that meant these crooks were bad news.

I took Miss B's cordless phone off its base and handed it to Howie. "Take this just in case," I said. "You go wait in the back alley."

Howie ran to the stockroom; I heard the back door slam behind him.

I locked the door that led from the stockroom into the store, then shoved a chair under the knob. Once I got those guys in, I wanted them to stay in.

When I made it to the alley, Howie was waiting, practicing his Miranda delivery.

"You have the right to remain silent . . . ," he recited. "If you choose to talk, anything you say can and will—"

"Hey, Howie," I said, "maybe you should peek into that Dumpster to see if there are any shipping boxes from the fake purses."

Howie knitted his brow. "Good idea. There may be tracking codes printed on them, and that will prove these guys have been at this a while."

"Here, I'll give you a boost."

I interlaced my fingers and Howie put his foot in my hands.

90

"Am I too heavy for you?" he asked.

I had to force myself not to laugh. "Um, no."

He bounced up to the rim of the Dumpster and peered over the side. "Zoe, you were right. There are lots of boxes in here with the R.A.D. logo printed on them."

"Are there any tracking numbers?" I asked, feeling guilty for what I was about to do.

"It's hard to tell. . . ."

"Then how about a closer look?" I said, giving a slight boost with my hands. Howie toppled into the Dumpster.

"ZOE!"

"Oops! Howie, I'm so sorry. I don't know how that happened."

Just then, a van came rumbling down the alley.

"What now?" Howie demanded, his voice echoing in the deep metal Dumpster. "You can't tackle them on your own! Get me out of here!"

"There's no time!" I replied. "Look, I'll get them into the stockroom and lock the door behind them. You have the cell phone, don't you? Well, call my dad at the station and tell him to come down to the boutique right now. But whatever you do, Howie, don't tell him I was here. He'd ground me for life if he knew I was messing around in police business again."

"I promise not to say a word."

I hid behind the Dumpster and listened to the rumbling get louder. Seconds later, the van pulled into the area near the stockroom door that served as the unloading zone for delivery trucks. I peeked out, keeping low in the hope that if they looked around, they'd look at adult head level and wouldn't see a kid crouched at knee level. Three burly men piled out of the front. One went to knock on the stockroom door. It swung open at his first rap.

"Hey, it ain't locked," he called.

"Maybe the old lady left it open for us."

The other two went around to the back of the van, opened the doors, and pulled out three giant boxes with R.A.D. logos crookedly stenciled on the sides. They walked awkwardly under the weight of the boxes, their fingers gripping the sides and their legs bowed out. I waited until the last in line—the one who had knocked on the stockroom door—had gotten a box and reached the doorway. Then I leaped out from behind the Dumpster.

The third guy whirled around. "Huh? Hey, kid . . ."

I ducked my head down like a football player and, using super-force, rammed my shoulder into his gut, sending him staggering into the stockroom. I heard a loud *ooompf!* as he crashed into one of the other goons, and they both tumbled to the floor.

"Jerks," I said, slamming the door and locking it tight. Then, for good measure, I gave the doorknob a supersqueeze, mangling the lock. It would take my dad and five policemen with crowbars to get these guys out.

CHAPTER 11

I came down to breakfast the next morning to find the kitchen table covered with fake R.A.D. BAGS.

"What's all this? Someone go on a shopping spree?" I said innocently. I had to play dumb, pretend I hadn't been anywhere near the boutique when the action went down.

Dad looked up from a bag he was tagging with a small paper ticket and grinned. "We busted a counterfeit crime ring last night," he said, writing a number on the ticket with a blue marker. "These are all knockoff bags confiscated from Miss Bettancourt's storeroom. She was upset to learn she'd been selling fakes, and I think the information she's giving us will help catch the rest of the gang. The delivery guys have also been singing like canaries in the hope of getting off lightly, so it won't be long before the whole gang is in police custody!"

I gave him my best confused expression, and he explained the whole situation, starting with Howie's data collation and finishing up with the amazing operation in the storeroom of Miss B's boutique. I alternated between looking surprised and impressed. Not a bad acting job, if I do say so myself.

"So what happens to all the fake bags?" I asked.

"Well, for the moment, they'll be entered into evidence and kept down at the station house to be used when the case against the counterfeiters goes to trial. There were so many of them that I offered to bring a couple of boxes home and inventory them." He chuckled. "Those guys in the evidence room are going to be up to their elbows in purses for the next couple of weeks."

I took extra long putting Pop-Tarts in the toaster to hide the broad grin on my face. My first major crime bust! I didn't even mind (much) that I couldn't share how I was feeling with Mom and Dad. I'd be able to tell Grandpa Zack as soon as he got back from the conference, and I might even make the *Superhero News*! Go, Kid Zoom!

On the way to school, Dad let me in on a secret.

"We're going to have a little send-off party for Officer Howie," he told me. "To thank him for all his hard work over these last two weeks."

"Great," I said. And it was great for Howie—he'd done some good detective work! But I wasn't thinking about the R.A.D. BAG triumph that much; the fact that I still had to face Electra was on my mind again.

She'd invaded my privacy by going through my backpack, and she'd put me in a really touchy situation by taking ideas from my grandfather's scrapbook. I still hadn't decided if I should mention it to her or not. If I did, I'd have to explain about my Super legacy. If I didn't, she'd publish those books featuring Zip's real-life Super adventures and the Federation would be very upset.

Thinking about it was giving me a stomachache. I leaned forward and turned on the radio, hoping to distract myself with some music.

"And now for the local weather report," came the announcer's voice. "Looks like Sweetbriar is in for severe atmospheric activity later today. Could get pretty wild, with heavy rain, thunderstorms, and wind gusts of up to sixty miles an hour."

"Gonna be rainy . . . ," I grumbled, pressing the next preset button on the radio. Traffic report. Next button—classical music. Yuck. The third button was the lucky one: a real bopping rock tune—my and Emily's current favorite—came blasting through the speakers.

By the time we reached school, I was in a much better mood. I turned down the radio as Dad pulled into the school driveway.

"So your work-study project wraps up today, huh?"

I nodded. "Yeah. It's done."

"Bet you learned a lot about comic books." He drove up to the curb to let me out. "Must have been a real adventure. I mean, not everybody gets to be part of the superhero experience for two whole weeks."

"True," I said with a wry smile. I grabbed my backpack, opened the door, and hopped out onto the sidewalk. "And you know what, Dad? I have a feeling the superhero experience is going to stay with me for a lifetime."

When Mr. Diaz dismissed us at twelve o'clock for our final afternoon of the apprenticeship program, I slid out the side door instead of leaving with everyone through the main lobby. I knew that Emily and Josh would be talking about what a great time they'd had doing their work-study jobs, and Howie had been on cloud nine all day, since his counterfeiting bust had been on the morning news. All the teachers and kids had congratulated him and made a big fuss over him. Even Caitlin seemed pretty happy about what she'd learned from Mr. Hunt at the flower shop.

I was happy for my friends—honest, I was. I just wasn't in the mood to celebrate, knowing that I was heading into a very awkward situation.

As I walked, I noticed that the day had gotten dark and the wind was picking up. I remembered vaguely that the weather forecast had been for stormy skies, but I was too busy trying to think of what I was going to say to Electra to recall the details.

I reached the front door of the mansion and clanged the bolt-shaped knocker. Seconds later the door swung open and there was Electra, holding a giant cake baked in the shape of a lightning bolt. One tall sparkler fizzled brightly in the center of it.

"For the world's best intern!" she cried, her eyes shining in the sparkler's glow.

Awkward much? Uh . . . *yes.*

I forced a smile. "Thanks," I said, stepping into the foyer. I followed her to the kitchen, where she put the cake on a high counter.

"Oh, Zoe," she said, bustling around collecting plates and forks and a large knife. "I really am going to miss having you around. I can't tell you how much I've enjoyed our time together."

I dropped my backpack on the floor, pulled a tall stool up to the counter, and sat down. "That's nice to hear," I said, feeling clunky and weird. Didn't she know that I *knew* what she'd done? Did she think I wouldn't care that she had violated my privacy? I didn't understand. She was acting so nice, so normal, like maybe . . .

"Hope you like chocolate," she said, cutting into the cake, carefully avoiding the still sparkling sparkler. She made three more cuts, then balanced the dainty square of cake on the blade of the knife. I held out my plate, but Electra shook her head.

"Oh, no. This little bitty calorie-conscious serving is for me," she said, sliding the small piece onto her plate. "This one is for you." She sliced into the cake again and produced an enormous, frosted chunk. She put it on my plate.

"Wow. That's a big one."

"Well, Zoe, you deserve a *super*sized piece!"

I froze, my fork poised above the yellow swirls of the frosting.

"Before I forget," Electra went on, licking a blob of frosting off her knuckle. "I've got your evaluation forms all ready to go."

She went to the fridge; there was an envelope secured to it with a lightning-bolt-shaped magnet. "Here you go. I think Marty Diaz will be very pleased with this. I'll mail it tomorrow."

Electra took a forkful of her cake.

I took one of mine.

The sparkler sputtered out. The room went eerily silent. I could hear the rain beating against the window, soft at first but growing stronger.

"Something wrong?" Electra asked at last.

"I was just wondering . . . I mean . . . well, that is . . ." I sighed and took another bite of cake, which I chewed slowly, stalling for time. "Ms. Allbright, how did you come up with all those neat ideas? The ones you were working on the day you sent me home. It felt like maybe you didn't want me to see them."

Electra looked at me in surprise. "Oh, no! I'm sorry if you felt left out, Zoe. It's just that I wasn't ready for you to see them *yet*!" She looked down at the small amount of cake left on her plate. "Artistic inspiration is a difficult thing to explain," she said quietly. "For some, it's imagination. For others, it's wishful thinking. For me, it's—"

At that moment, a jagged bolt of lightning lit up the sky. Thunder echoed, drowning out the end of what Electra was saying. By the time the rumble had faded to silence, she was heading for the stairs.

"Ready to get to work?" she called over her shoulder.

"Sure." I slid off the stool and followed her up to the attic. As we passed through the upstairs hall, I remembered how excited I'd been the first day, when Electra had shown me her studio. Back then I couldn't wait to hear about how she came up with her thrilling stories. Now I could hardly bear to think about it.

Things sure had changed.

Two hours later, I'd washed about forty ink bottles. It seemed an especially appropriate task today. The sound of the water running in the sink blended sadly with the rain outside, and the inky colors ran together, turning the water a swirly blue-green-gray, like the stormy sky. Like my mood.

Finally, I put the last ink bottle in the cupboard and closed the door.

"That's the last one," I said.

"Oh." Electra looked up from a page she was coloring and gave me a sad smile. "Well, then, I guess your work here is done."

"Guess so." I cleared my throat. "So . . . yeah. Well, thanks for everything."

"You're very welcome."

Why did you do it? Why did you lie?

I wanted to ask. I didn't want to ask. I knew I had every right, but at the same time I couldn't help wondering, *What would be the point?* Electra hadn't told me about her new storyboard while she worked and I washed. But she hadn't tried to conceal it from me, either. As I'd moved around the attic, collecting dirty bottles and searching for more detergent, I'd caught glimpses of the work. The story was an awful lot like the ones in my grandfather's scrapbook, but she'd changed his name from Zip to Vroom. Actually, it looked as if she'd taken several of the stories and blended them together.

I hoped Super exposure wasn't a concern, since the comic was technically a fictional story, but that didn't stop me from feeling disappointed and betrayed.

In the end, I just couldn't bring myself to ask why she'd done it—stolen my grandfather's stories for her comics. Probably because deep down, I knew I wouldn't like the answer.

Even though it was my last day, the hours really dragged. At last it was four-thirty and I could go home. I crossed the attic toward the door just as a violent gust of wind rattled the windows.

"Getting pretty nasty out there," Electra observed. "I think I should drive you home."

"No, that's okay."

"But Zoe, it's—"

"Really. I'm fine. I've got an umbrella."

Electra looked as if she wanted to argue, but in the end she just smiled. "All right then."

I left the attic, pounded down the two flights of stairs to the kitchen, grabbed my backpack, and ran out the door.

I didn't look back.

CHAPTER 12

I trudged through Sweetbriar, barely aware of the force of the wind that whipped against my face and through my hair. If I hadn't had superstrength, it would have knocked me over. I just kept my head low and walked with firm strides into the fury of the storm. The rain pelted me like little steel balls, and thunder exploded again and again behind the clouds.

I could have made the trip home at superspeed since there was no traffic to speak of; the weather seemed to be keeping people indoors. I could have run, but for maybe the first time since I'd found out about my powers, I just didn't feel like using them. It suited my mood to walk as slowly as a regular person and get completely soaked.

I was nearing the Sweetbriar River. The high metal bridge that crossed the deepest part of the river had just come into sight when the most brilliant flash of lightning I'd ever seen lit up the darkened sky. That got my attention! I raised my eyes to the gray-black clouds in time to see a long, jagged blade of lightning strike the tall electrical tower that stood on the far side of the river, just beside the bridge. A huge crackling and hissing noise burst from the tower and a shower of sparks sprang to life, slicing through the midsection of the narrow metal structure.

I gasped and ducked, covering my head with my arms. There was a weird—and yucky—burning smell, and I could feel the hairs on my arms standing up from all the electricity in the air.

Behind me, I heard the sound of an engine, followed by the screech of brakes, but I couldn't look; my eyes were glued to the top portion of the tower, which was swaying, severing itself from the base. Its long tentacle-like electrical wires flailed against the angry sky, sputtering and buzzing, shooting off more sparks. I was aware of more screeching coming from behind me—the desperate sound of someone slamming on the brakes and not being able to stop—and I whirled around to see that a school bus from Sweetbriar Elementary was skidding straight toward the side of the bridge. The driver must have seen the electrical tower get hit by the lightning and tried to stop before reaching the bridge, but the road was covered in at least two inches of rainwater and his brakes were useless. The bus barreled onto the bridge just as the electrical tower came toppling down.

My first thought was to jump up and catch the falling tower. But I wasn't wearing my supersuit and I had no idea if an out-of-uniform superhero could be electrocuted. My guess was yes. Hadn't I just gotten a major shock from wearing new slippers on my bedroom carpet last week?

I could catch the bus and carry it safely to the opposite side of the bridge, but I was bound to be seen.

As these thoughts raced through my brain at warp speed, I watched the bus swerve to avoid being crushed by the falling, spark-spewing chunk of metal tower, which had just hit the surface of the bridge. In the space of a heartbeat, I heard the bus tires squealing on the wet pavement, and stared as the long yellow vehicle skidded sideways toward the thick metal guardrail of the bridge.

The sound of the impact was almost unbearable—metal grinding against metal as the bus came to a hard stop against the rail. The weight of the bus bent the rail to the point that it looked ready to snap like a Popsicle stick.

ZOE, DO SOMETHING!

Moving faster than the lightning itself, I flung myself behind a mailbox and dug into my backpack for my suit. I peeled off my wet clothes and wriggled into the suit just as a megagust lifted the mailbox from the sidewalk and into the sky.

I ran for the bridge.

The bus was shimmying in the strong wind; the girders of the bridge were creaking loudly as it struggled against the wind, and the rail was straining under the weight of the vehicle. As I ran toward the bus, I could hear the kids inside screaming for help. I figured screaming was better than no sound at all.

The door of the bus was crumpled against the guardrail, pinning the driver into his seat. The windows on that side were over the river, so the children couldn't climb out of them. Some of the kids were struggling to open the windows on the bridge side, but they were little and scared, and without the bus driver to help them, they couldn't figure out how to release the safety glass. The broken tower slid closer and closer to their bus, pushed along by the force of the gale. Its live electrical wires reared up like giant snakes, snapping like whips toward the bus, throwing sparks into the air every time they moved.

I know from science class that cars and buses can ordinarily withstand electrical currents because the rubber of the tires acts as a ground. But the fact that the bus was pressed against a metal guardrail was a problem. The rail would act as a conductor, overriding the grounding effect of the tires. So if the electric wires made contact, the current would shoot straight through the bus—and the kids.

The first thing I had to do was move the broken tower and its wires, which were scooting ever closer to the bus.

No. The first thing to do was to move the bus away from the broken rail. Then the rubber tires would save the kids inside from the electrical cables.

But what if the wires struck the bus before I could get a good grip on it? I should get rid of the tower first.

But what if the rail gave way while I was moving the tower? The bus, with all those kids and the driver inside, would fall over the edge and into the rushing river, which seemed to be rising by the second.

My pulse was racing. I tried to tell myself not to freak out, to stay calm, to think clearly. Just then, a clap of thunder made the bridge shudder under my feet, as though the universe were urging me to act, and fast. There was no time to stop and think clearly. But so much depended on my doing things in the right order. So much . . .

"Arrrrghhh!" I let out a shout of frustration. "What do I do first?"

A bolt of lightning illuminated the sky.

And I heard someone shout at me:

"Chronology is always the toughest part."

I turned to see someone wearing a glittering eye mask and an impressive yellow outfit. It was clearly not as new as mine; Emily might even call it retro. The pants had giant bell-bottoms and the top had huge cuffs and lapels. It looked . . . well, the only word I could think of to describe it was *groovy*. Her hands were on her hips; her legs were braced apart.

"Lightning Girl?" I cried in disbelief.

"Close enough," the yellow-clad figure replied.

I gasped as I recognized the voice, then smiled. "Electra!"

My comic-book mentor and fellow superhero smiled. "We don't have time to talk right now," she called over the noise of the rain. "You grab the bus. I'll handle the wires! *Go!*"

It was way easier with two superheroes.

I crouched at the back of the bus, slid my hands underneath it, and lifted it with only the slightest effort. I had to be careful not to tilt it too much because I didn't want to send all the kids shooting to the other end.

Walking quickly—and as smoothly as I could, given the cir-cumstances—across the swaying bridge, I carried the bus to the solid ground on the other side. Then I ducked out of sight behind a billboard to watch Electra do her thing. The short, spiky blond hair, the musical lilt to the voice—I'd been working side by side with this person for two weeks. I knew it with certainty: Lightning Girl was real . . . and she was Electra Allbright.

I watched her grab the live wires (without even flinching) and tie them off into a neat bow, as if she were wrapping a present, then lift the hunk of twisted metal and fly it away from the bridge, where she deposited it safely on the ground. It only took her a couple of seconds, and she looked so efficient and . . . and . . . experienced while she was doing it! I could still hardly believe I was watching my mentor.

When Electra joined me behind the billboard, I could hear rescue sirens in the distance.

"Let's get out of here," she suggested. "I think we have some things to discuss."

I nodded, suddenly feeling worn out to the ends of my toes.

She hooked her arm around my waist, careful not to dig my tool belt into my side. With the dark clouds roiling above us, we flew back to her house.

I was sitting at the counter in Electra's kitchen again, just as I'd done every weekday afternoon for the past two weeks—only this time, I was dressed in an indestructible supersuit.

And so was she.

She'd made hot cocoa for the two of us; the chocolatey smell filled the kitchen while the rain carried on hammering at the windowpanes.

Electra picked up a can of whipped cream, shook it, then poised the spout over my steaming cocoa. "Say when," she instructed.

I let her continue to swirl the cream into the cup until she'd created a fat white mountain.

"When."

She shook the can again, then put twice as much cream into her own cup. "I think I burned enough calories this afternoon to justify this."

We sipped in silence for a while.

"Well," she said at last, "I might as well start at the beginning."

"That would be good," I said, resting my elbows on the counter.

"I was a working superhero for many, many years. Like you, I received my powers on my twelfth birthday. I was known as Electra Girl."

"Not Lightning Girl?" I interrupted, puzzled.

Electra laughed. "Anonymity, remember? Anonymity and poetic license, actually. I think Lightning Girl sounds much better! I had—well, *have*—the power to generate electrical currents, as well as to withstand high voltage—and to fly, of course. My uncle Illuminoe trained me. Once I was ready to undertake missions, I got in with a very elite Super crowd, let me tell you. We were the best of the best."

"I think my grandpa Zack was part of that crowd," I said, recalling the articles I'd read in his scrapbook. After all, how many superhero elites could there be? There weren't very many of us in the first place.

Electra nodded, and her eyes looked kind of dreamy. "Zip. He was a hero even among heroes. We went on a lot of missions together back then. We were a good team."

Her voice had definitely gotten softer when she was talking about Zack. I was dying to ask her if she and Grandpa had ever been boyfriend and girlfriend before he met my grandma, but I just couldn't bring myself to do it. Thinking back to the times I'd seen them interact in the dry cleaner's, and the day at the ice cream shop, though, I had my suspicions. And then there was the tension between her and my grandma—Gran acted exactly like someone would behave around her husband's old sweetheart. Whoa, this was turning out to be way more information about my family legacy than I had bargained for!

"The comic-book thing came about quite by accident," Electra went on, taking us back to a less personal topic, much to my relief. "It wasn't that I didn't enjoy my superhero job. I did, very much. Saved this planet more times than I can count. Went all over the world . . . saw everything I'd ever want to see, and plenty of things I'd rather I hadn't seen. On my fiftieth birthday, after a rather amazing bash thrown for me by the Superhero Federation, I sat down and took stock of my life. After deep thought and long deliberation, I came to this profound conclusion: I was tired. Just plain tired." She paused to sip her cocoa.

I smiled, remembering how I'd felt the day I saved the little boy from the tiger, not to mention just moments ago, after we'd moved the bus. "Yeah," I said. "I can relate." Maybe too many days like that would get to you in the end. Not that I was in any hurry to get through my next thirty-eight years of superheroism!

"The funny thing was that while I was sitting there thinking and deliberating, I had picked up a marker and begun doodling. Without even realizing it, I had covered several pages, depicting my superhero beginnings. And that's when I knew what I wanted to do. The next day, I submitted a letter of resignation to the Superhero Federation and submitted my doodle pages to an editor at Fusion Comics.

"Well, the editor loved my concept and bought the series. The Federation, on the other hand, had a less enthusiastic response. They were okay with my retiring, but they absolutely forbade me to publish a comic book about my adventures."

"Why?" I asked. "No one would ever believe they were based on your real-life experiences. People read about Superman and Spider-Man and no one believes they're real." I raised an eyebrow. "They're not real, are they?"

Electra laughed. "Pure fiction. Which was what I tried to tell the Federation. But they were afraid someone out there would figure out that the superheroes I was writing about really existed. Well, I'd been a hero long enough to respect their decision, so although LG number one had already been published, I had to pull it from circulation."

"So that's why no one can find it!" I said, thinking of the hours Connie at Connie's Cosmic Comic Shop had spent searching for that one particular issue. "So what happened? How come you published the rest of the series?"

"I had to promise to be very careful not to give too much away. I could use my own adventures as inspiration, but I could never use real superhero names or descriptions."

"I have to ask . . . ," I began, placing my empty cocoa mug on the counter. "The other day when you sent me home—was it because you had snooped through my backpack and used my grandpa's scrapbook for inspiration for all those storyboards?"

Electra didn't seem at all angry at the accusation. Instead, she held up her hand and used her pinky to trace a lightning bolt over her heart—the Lightning Girl pledge sign. "I promise you, Zoe, I did not look in your backpack."

"But the storyboards were almost identical to the adventures I read about in Grandpa's books."

"Well, there's a good reason for that. You see, Zoe, you remind me so much of your grandfather that having you around these past two weeks has made me very nostalgic. It really got me thinking more and more about the old days, and I started remembering a whole bunch of adventures I hadn't thought about in years. I didn't have to look at those books to know about those missions, because I was there for most of them."

I wanted to hug her! She hadn't betrayed me after all. Then another question came to me.

"If you retired all those years ago, why did you use your powers today?"

Electra blushed. "To tell you the truth, lately I've missed the hero gig, and I'm thinking about asking the Feds to reinstate me. Zack seems to be having such a wonderful time training you— I guess I wanted to get my hand back into the rescue game."

It occurred to me that Electra didn't have a grandchild of her own to train. "You never got married?" I said, hoping it wasn't too personal a question.

"Never found the right guy," she replied softly. "I came close once, but it didn't work out and he found someone else. Someone perfect for him."

I wanted to ask who that almost right guy had been . . . but I didn't.

Electra looked out the window. The rain had almost stopped, and the wind had died down to a vigorous breeze. "C'mon, Kid Zoom. Let's get you home."

CHAPTER 13

MY parents were a nervous wreck.

I wasn't surprised. They worried about me when the weather was perfect—naturally they were in major panic mode to think I could be out somewhere in that crazy storm.

"Where have you been?" Mom cried, throwing her arms around me as soon as I walked through the door.

I let her hug me and didn't even complain. It had been a rough day and I needed a little TLC. I was back in my school clothes now; I'd changed out of my supersuit at Electra's house before she drove me home.

"We tried calling you at Electra's, but the storm knocked out the phone lines. Daddy sent a police cruiser over there, but they said no one answered the door."

"Her studio is in the attic," I said, thinking fast. "I guess with all the thunder and wind and being all the way up on the top floor, we never heard them at the door."

When Mom finished hugging me, Dad came over and hugged me, too.

"I'm just so glad you're home safe." His voice was troubled. "When I think of all those children on that school bus, and how badly they could have been hurt . . ."

"School bus?" I echoed, opening my eyes wide. I'm getting used to acting like I don't know about some things. "What school bus?"

That night Grandpa and Gran came for dinner, fresh from their vacation, with suntanned faces and lots of presents.

While Mom and Dad cleared the table, I sat in the living room with my grandparents.

"I heard you had a busy week," Grandpa said, straightening the giant sequined sombrero I was wearing, my favorite souvenir from their trip.

"How did you hear?"

"Thatcher and I go way back," he replied. "I had a whole string of messages from him when I got home."

Gran raised her eyebrows at me. "And what about the bus that almost went over the bridge during the storm? The one I heard about on the news on our drive home." I could tell from her voice that she'd already guessed I'd been involved.

"Was that you?" Grandpa asked, his face filled with pride.

"Er, kind of. Me and . . . Electra Girl."

I looked from Grandpa Zack to Gran, then back to Grandpa. They both looked totally shocked.

"It's okay, I know all about her," I went on. "How she was a great hero in her day, and how she retired and how the Federation got angry over the comic books."

"But Electra has been classified inactive for decades," Grandpa said.

"Well, she wants to become active again. She misses the excitement and she misses helping the world."

"She always was an unpredictable one," Gran said, shaking her head.

I was glad to hear Gran describe Electra as unpredictable and not . . . well, something worse. I wasn't exactly sure where we all stood at the moment. It seemed as if maybe Gran felt kind of jealous about Electra and Zip's past connection. And I was afraid Grandpa might be angry with me for working with her without his (or the Federation's) permission. And then there was the whole comic-book thing. I decided I might as well address that issue here and now.

"While we're on the subject of Electra," I began carefully, "why didn't you just tell me who Electra was from the beginning?"

Grandpa sighed. "I've been mistrustful of Electra since the whole comic-book brouhaha," he said. "I was afraid that if you knew, you might be tricked into telling her all your superhero secrets."

"But she would never do anything to endanger me . . . or any of us. She's a real hero at heart. And now that I've worked with her, I can tell you for sure that the comic books aren't as bad as you think. She really doesn't give away anything about the real heroes. Sure, she draws from her experiences, but she changes the names and swaps the powers around. You'd never know they were real stories unless . . . well, unless you *knew* they were real stories, like we do."

116

I could tell from Grandpa's expression that he wasn't ready to accept that yet. I knew him well enough to know that if he had reservations, they were probably for good reason. This was not an issue that was going to be ironed out in one quick discussion. I'd just have to wait and see.

Then Mom and Dad came in with a tray of coffee and dessert and the conversation turned to Gran and Grandpa's not so super but very entertaining adventures on the cruise ship.

After my grandparents left, I went upstairs. It had been a crazy day; I needed some time on my own. And there was something I wanted to do.

I sat down at my computer and wrote an addition to my Superhero Federation essay. I would e-mail it to the Federation and tell them I wasn't looking for extra credit or anything—but then again, if they wanted to give me some bonus points, I wasn't about to argue.

> One of the things I learned from studying my ancestry was that the most important power a Super can have is the power of family . . . and the power of friends. Even if a superhero has the ability to save the world all on her own, it's much nicer to have someone working beside you. Many hands make light work, as they say. So I guess many Super hands make superlight work.

I read it over, feeling pleased, then got down to the other business at hand: my work-study report. I had totally forgotten about it in the confusion of thinking that Electra had betrayed me and fearing that I'd exposed the whole superhero community!

It wasn't going to be easy to write. There was so much to think about—for example, how I now had two completely different pictures of Electra Allbright in my head. There was Electra the writer—a hip, chatty, fabulously creative woman who created comic books—and Electra Girl, the superpowered crime fighter. I wished I could mention both Electras in my report, but of course, I couldn't.

Settling in for yet another report-writing session, I pulled out a piece of loose-leaf paper and began.

On Monday, Mr. Diaz called us up one at a time to give our reports. All my classmates had visual aids and cool props that had to do with their jobs.

All except me. In the rush to save a busload of schoolkids on Friday, I hadn't had a chance to ask Electra for anything like that—no storyboard, no sample comic pages, not even a freshly washed ink bottle. I felt annoyed with myself for forgetting about the presentation, but it was too late to do anything about it now.

Howie went first, telling us all about the brave work done by the Sweetbriar Police. Then my dad arrived with the chief, and they awarded Howie a special medal for his part in bringing down the counterfeit handbag ring.

When Howie passed my desk on his way back to his own seat,

he gave me an apologetic look. I could tell he felt bad that I wasn't getting any of the credit. But I'd sworn him to secrecy about my being at the boutique, and I knew Howie was going to keep his promise. I gave him a wink and a thumbs-up. I promised myself I'd tell him that I really didn't mind, and that I was just as proud of him as everyone else was, since he'd done all the investigating that led to the arrest.

Next, Caitlin gave a flower-arranging demonstration using chrysanthemums and roses. Unfortunately, Ethan Danvers, who'd done his apprenticeship at the ice cream shop, turned out to be highly allergic to chrysanthemums and sneezed through his whole report, which included a sundae-making lesson. At the end of the demo, he offered the sundae to Mr. Diaz, who (since Ethan had sneezed on it at least fifty times) politely declined.

Josh's presentation was a big hit. He brought in an aquarium-sized glass tank filled with insects. Allison Newkirk nearly fainted when he put it on her desk, but other than that, everyone enjoyed seeing all the weird bugs. I couldn't help thinking that he was a lot braver than I am around creepy-crawlies! As Josh headed back to his desk, he gave me a grin over the top of the tank. I blushed so hard it felt as if my cheeks were fizzing.

Emily talked about the fast-paced world of magazine publishing and gave us some helpful fashion tips to get us through that difficult spring-to-summer wardrobe transition period.

And then it was my turn.

I slid out of my desk and walked to the front of the room.

"I did my apprenticeship with Electra Allbright," I said, "author and illustrator of the Lightning Girl comics. Um . . . I learned a lot about—"

A knock on the classroom door interrupted me. Mr. Diaz

opened it and someone in the hall handed him a large cardboard box. He opened the lid, peeked inside, and smiled at what he saw.

"I believe these are for you, Zoe," he said, bringing the box to the front of the room.

I looked inside and gasped. Smiling broadly, I reached into the box and pulled out what had to be just about the coolest thing I'd ever seen.

There were enough copies for the whole class. So proud I felt like bursting, I began passing them out. Everyone oohed and aahed as they flipped through the pages. The comic-book-character Zoe looked just like me, of course. Electra had drawn her flying, and shooting electricity from her fingertips and making herself invisible, all while she did various tasks and chores in a comic-book artist's studio! But there was no need for Grandpa Zack to worry. None of my actual powers was illustrated—in the interest of secrecy and security. Hey, now I was a comic-book superhero as well as a real one!

I passed out all the comic books, putting the final one down on Josh's desk. He looked at the cartoon version of me and grinned. "You make a great superhero," he said.

"Thanks!" I said with a smile. "I'd like to think so. Too bad it's only make-believe."

But even as I said it, I felt a tiny thrill knowing that I'll be putting this comic book into *my* scrapbook, and someday, years from now, a twelve-year-old superhero will have a chance to read it. My grandkid, maybe. The next Super from the Richards family.

HOW COOL IS THAT?

ZOE QUINN lives in Maryland with her family and still loves reading comic books. She is the author of two previous books in the Caped Sixth Grader series, *Happy Birthday, Hero!* and *Totally Toxic.*